SECOND CHANCE WITH HIS SUNSHINE SURGEON

AMY RUTTAN

Recycling programs for this product may not exist in your area

ISBN-13: 978-1-335-99369-4

Second Chance with His Sunshine Surgeon

For questions and comments about the quality of this book, please contact us at CustomerService@Harlequin.com.

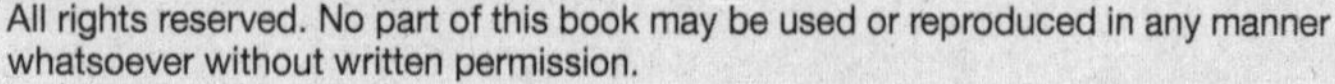

Harlequin Enterprises ULC
22 Adelaide St. West, 41st Floor
Toronto, Ontario M5H 4E3, Canada
www.Harlequin.com

HarperCollins Publishers
Macken House, 39/40 Mayor Street Uppe
Dublin 1, D01 C9W8, Ireland
www.HarperCollins.com

Printed in U.S.A.

1 2 3 4 5 6 7 8 9 10 HDC 28 27 26 25

"Would you like to have lunch with me?" Emile asked. "I think we have some more things to discuss."

Chloé's eyes widened. "Do we?"

"About the case." What had come over him? He never went out to lunch with anyone. Actually, he never really took a lunch break at all. It must just have been habit, because when they'd been residents they always ate together.

"Sure," Chloé said. "It's a date." Pink bloomed in her cheeks. "I mean...lunch. Business lunch."

"Bonne." Emile turned on his heel and left, quickly, putting some space between them. He wasn't going to change his mind about lunch, but he was annoyed that he'd put the invite out there anyway.

This was not maintaining a working relationship.

This was not keeping his distance.

Dear Reader,

Thank you for picking up Chloé and Emile's story, *Second Chance with His Sunshine Surgeon*.

I love being able to set books in my beautiful country of Canada. It's been a long time since I've been to Montreal, but it's a place I would love to revisit as an adult. Last time I was there was a grade 8 field trip!

Chloé has a sunny personality, which hides her own pain from losing her twin sister years ago. What I love about her is how she dedicated her life to help others, and the passion in her work. Although I'm not as sunshiny as Chloé, she's just been a wonderful character to write.

Emile is closed off, a bit of a grump, but he absolutely melts when he's around Chloé, and I just love broody heroes like that. I've always loved a Mr. Darcy type of hero, and Emile is no exception.

I also love reunion/second chance romances, so it was a lot of fun to explore that again.

I hope you enjoy Chloé and Emile's story!

I love hearing from readers, so please drop by my website, amyruttan.com.

With warmest wishes,

Amy Ruttan

Born and raised just outside Toronto, Ontario, **Amy Ruttan** fled the big city to settle down with the country boy of her dreams. After the birth of her second child, Amy was lucky enough to realize her lifelong dream of becoming a romance author. When she's not furiously typing away at her computer, she's mom to three wonderful children, who use her as a personal taxi and chef.

Books by Amy Ruttan

Harlequin Medical Romance

Caribbean Island Hospital

Reunited with Her Surgeon Boss
A Ring for His Pregnant Midwife

Portland Midwives

The Doctor She Should Resist

Falling for His Runaway Nurse
Paramedic's One-Night Baby Bombshell
Winning the Neonatal Doc's Heart
Nurse's Pregnancy Surprise
Reunited with Her Off-Limits Surgeon
Tempted by the Single Dad Next Door
Rebel Doctor's Boston Reunion
Snowbound with the Single Mom

Visit the Author Profile page
at Harlequin.com for more titles.

This book is for one of the most sunshiny people
I know, TL! You always brighten my day,
even on some particularly cloudy ones.
Thanks for forcing your way into my life
and deciding I was going to be your friend.

CHAPTER ONE

I FEEL LIKE *he's watching me.*

Although, Dr. Emile Moreau felt that way every time he passed his father's venerable portrait that was hanging on the Moreau hospital wing of Hôpital de Ville-Marie. One in a *very* long line of Moreaus that adorned the memorial wall. Each and every one of his ancestors staring down at him with an almost righteous indignation. Even though Emile walked these halls every day, for most of his life, and even though his father had died while he was still in medical school, he could still feel his father's eyes boring into the back of his skull from that damnable photograph.

Judging him.

Displeased with him.

And disappointed.

"*If you want to be the best and save lives, you have to toughen up. Your work is your life. It comes first. Nothing else matters.*" His father's voice echoing in his mind. It weighed heavy on him. A burden he just couldn't escape.

It didn't help that Hôpital de Ville-Marie's cardiac wing only existed thanks to his late grandfather's philanthropic endeavors. Then his father's brilliance in the cardiothoracic surgical field had built the reputation that meant people came from all over Montreal to get the very best in care.

Emile's care now.

He stiffened his spine and adjusted his tie.

His late father and he had not had a loving relationship, but Dr. Moreau Senior had been brilliant and that was why Emile had followed in his footsteps. Really, there were no other options for him. He was a Moreau and the only possible path for a Moreau was cardiothoracic medicine.

Emile had even surpassed his father in one way, by becoming the youngest head of cardiothoracic surgery at Hôpital de Ville-Marie.

Not that it would have pleased his father. No matter what Emile did, nothing had ever seemed to make him happy.

So he ignored the photographs and continued his brisk pace to his office. He knew exactly why he was feeling the weight of their gazes so strongly today; that was no mystery. And it wasn't only because he was still reeling from what he'd just seen on the imaging of one of his younger patients.

It was the fact that after ten years, he was going to have to call the only woman he ever loved, the one whom he had to let go, and ask her for help.

He passed a resident, who greeted him politely. Emile nodded stiffly at her and the group of nervous interns who were moving together quickly with her. He didn't give them a smile, but inside he was laughing slightly, remembering what it had been like when he was in their shoes.

That was when he'd been with Chloé. Those had been some of the happiest moments of his life.

And he'd never forgotten them. They just stayed buried, deep in his heart. His first love was and would always be Hôpital de Ville-Marie. Just like it had been for all those Moreaus who had come before him.

His mother still cursed this hospital's name.

Emile didn't blame her for that. There had been times as a young boy he did, too.

But he had learned where his cold, aloof father hadn't. There was no time for love, friendship, marriage or a family when you were running an illustrious cardiothoracic wing. And there was no way Emile would ever think of having a wife and starting a family just to ignore them or put them second because of work.

He couldn't pretend that he wasn't lonely sometimes, but he wasn't selfish. Sometimes you just couldn't have it all.

"These scans are in, Doctor Moreau," his assistant said as he entered his office. Donna had been his father's assistant before she'd been Emile's right-hand woman. She must be close to retirement now. He didn't know what he'd do once she left; she was the only one in this hospital who didn't shrink back in fear from him.

Not that Emile was a heartless person. His patients trusted him, and he always tried to be warm with them, but to run an efficient unit, he expected perfection and demanded respect from his staff.

And it was easier to keep most people at bay, rather than forge relationships with people who were most likely to leave as soon as a better opportunity arose.

Just like Chloé.

Emile shook that thought from his head. "*Merci*, Donna. When the call comes in from the hospital in Ottawa, please patch it through straightaway."

"I will, Doctor Moreau."

Emile retreated to the safety of his closed office and sat down at his desk, pulling up the images from the scan that had taken place last night. The premier of the province had brought in her child yesterday. The little girl had been presenting all the symptoms of heart failure, but there were irregularities—something else at play.

Emile had seen to the scans personally, so he'd known the moment the images came up what was happening.

Heart cancer.

It was rare and he didn't see many cases. He'd seen them in pathology in medical school, but not in the case of a child of six. The truth of the matter was he hadn't done many heart cancer surgeries in the first place and definitely not on someone so small. It was a risky surgery at the best of times, especially for someone without much experience.

Thankfully, he knew someone who had plenty.

The phone buzzed. He picked it up. "Yes, Donna?"

"Doctor Chloé MacDonald is on line one," Donna replied.

"*Merci.*" His pulse was pounding between his ears as he took a deep breath and connected to the call. "Doctor MacDonald."

"Oh, that's so formal," came the bright voice he knew all too well on the other end. "How are you, Doctor Moreau?"

He tried not to smile, although he could almost hear the air quotes as Chloé said his last name. "I am well. I trust by now you've seen the scans and my report?"

"Getting down to business, eh?"

"My time is…limited." He would've said *valuable*, but given Chloé's expertise as a surgeon, he knew her time was just as precious as his own.

"Limited. So obviously, we're done with pleasantries or friendly chatter."

Emile sighed and rubbed his temple. "It's a pressing issue."

"I'm well aware," she responded. "That's clear from the details you sent over."

"What do you think?"

"The child is six?" Chloé asked with some trepidation.

"*Oui.*"

"She's young for someone with this type of tumor."

"I know. You have worked on a case like this before, though."

"You keeping tabs on me?" Chloé teased.

He rolled his eyes. She still had the same sunshine-y personality he remembered so well. When he'd first met her that bubbliness had vexed him, but at the same time it had drawn him in. It had been such a departure from the strict, humorless household he'd grown up in.

Right now, though, he found it somewhat annoying because he needed to keep her at arm's length. He didn't want to be sucked back in, to be enchanted by her and the promise of warmth and joy that he had found with her once. That was not an efficient way to stay at the top of his game.

"Your career is impressive. So yes, I have kept tabs on you."

In truth, he'd tried not to, tried to block her memory from his life, but it was hard when her name was everywhere in medical journals. Her work and her research were testament to her dedication, as was her role as a persistent advocate for a better health infrastructure in remote northern communities.

It was what he'd always loved about Chloé; she had huge goals, just like him. The only difference was that he knew she wanted an equal partner, a family. They'd discussed it before, when they were dating and things had seemed like they were starting to get serious. Emile had told her then that he didn't want a family—a slight lie, but also not. Though part of him longed for one, he just couldn't commit to it. Work would always be more important and he couldn't ever hurt a child, a partner, by putting them second.

Chloé came from a loving home. He knew she had a supportive, happy childhood and wanted to provide the same for children of her own. That was a kind of life he didn't know how to give her.

The last thing he ever wanted to do was to make Chloé resent him the way his mother bitterly resented his father. As much as he was drawn to her, he had to resist. It would be painful, but it was the only way.

"I can hear your teeth grinding," she chuckled.

Emile relaxed. "Do you think you can help? I mean, does your schedule afford you the time to help us out in this situation? The child is very fragile, medically, and I don't know if transporting her would be in her best interest right now."

"No. You're right, if what I've read from her labs is correct," Chloé agreed. "It's best I come there."

"And you can fit this into your schedule?"

"I can," she replied brightly.

"Good. The board of directors has arranged a suite in a hotel where we often put our visiting physicians."

"You've already spoken to the board, eh? Seems like you've already decided for me," she teased.

"This is an urgent situation."

Emile heard her sigh down the line. "I do understand that. Well, send me all the information and arrangements and I'll hop in my car and make the trip. It's not a terribly long drive."

"No. It's not," he said tightly.

When their relationship had ended, it was partly because Chloé had taken her first job in Yellowknife and had been talking about moving back to her home city of Iqaluit. It had hurt him a little bit to see she only stayed in Yellowknife for six months, before moving to Ottawa, much closer to Montreal.

Maybe they could've worked things out had she gone to Ottawa in the first place.

Really? It wouldn't have worked out for plenty of reasons, and you know it.

Which was true. Emile needed to devote all his time and energy here, at the hospital. Proving he was the best, good enough to fill his father's shoes. Besides, he had never wanted to hold her back from her dreams. His destiny, his future, had all been planned for him. She had the opportunity to live out her life the way she wanted to. He didn't.

"Good, because the sooner I'm there, the quicker we can start treatment. This is an aggressive cancer."

"I will send the details over straightaway. I… I look forward to working with you again, Chloé." He hoped she didn't hear the hesitation in his voice, because there was a part of him that was nervous about seeing her again.

Just like there was a part of him that was excited about that prospect, too.

Don't think like that.

"And I you, Emile." Chloé disconnected the call.

Emile hung up the phone and sat back in his office chair, rubbing his hands over his face, before staring out at the city of Montreal spread out before him. From this vantage point in the hospital, he could see the gorgeous skyline of the city rising below him, and the St. Lawrence River winding its way from Lake Saint Louis—or really, its starting point at Lake Ontario over two hundred and eighty kilometers to the west—between the island of Île Notre-Dame and St. Helen's, under the Victoria bridge and eventually making its way out to the Atlantic Ocean.

Emile loved that sprawling river. When he was a child, his mother would always take him up the coast and into Québec City, where old-European style met with Canada. They would pick berries along the roads and always end up sharing a tortiere, picnicking under the roar of the Montmorency Falls.

Those halcyon days had come before his parents divorced. Before his dad got full custody and his mother moved to Beaupré. Before Emile and his mother became distant with each other. She didn't understand his passion for medicine, and he didn't understand her bohemian lifestyle.

Still, Québec had always been his home. He'd even gone to school here, but chosen to do his medical schooling in Toronto. Other than that, he hadn't wandered far from his roots, because what was the point of that? His father had set his path for him, right here.

Emile knew his place and yet, there were still times he wondered about the what-ifs.

What if he hadn't followed in his father's footsteps?

What if he had taken that fellowship in Vancouver?

What if he hadn't ended it with Chloé?

"I think it's for the best, cherie." It was hard to get those words out. He knew by the pain in his heart, the lump in his throat. "You want things I can't give you."

"Like what?" Chloé stood before him, her dark eyes moist with tears. The lips he loved to kiss, set firm in a straight line.

The body that had melted against his time and time again, stiff.

He'd hurt her.

"Family and career. You need someone to support your aspirations. I have my own goals. I have to be selfish."

"Selfish?"

"Oui."

"Why do you want to go to Montreal?" she asked. "And to your late father's hospital? Vancouver is offering you so much more."

It was a legitimate question, but one Emile didn't want to answer. "Why do you want to go to Iqaluit?"

"It's where I'm from. I'm needed there."

"Exactly."

"I'm not going there yet. I had an opportunity in Yellowknife. One that is offering me more so I can return home one day."

She was right, but there was no point in arguing or dragging it on. He took a deep breath. "Chloé."

She held up a hand. "No. Don't. I guess we really didn't promise each other anything. It was casual."

"Yes. Casual." He loved her, but he'd never told her that and now there was no point. It was time to let her go.

"I wish you the best, Doctor Moreau."

He nodded. "And I wish the same for you, Doctor MacDonald."

That was all in the past.

They'd gone their separate ways and forged the careers they wanted. Even though Emile had never forgotten her, this situation wasn't about that. This was about working together to save a young life, nothing more.

There was no way he was going to let those old feelings creep back in. He was over her.

Her time in his hospital would be temporary and then she'd be gone again.

Surely, enough water had gone under the bridge that he wouldn't be tempted by her again. At least, that was what he had to keep telling himself. For however long Chloé would be here, he had to keep his walls up and his heart closed.

Like he did with everyone else.

It had taken a couple of days for Chloé to get everything in order and head to Montreal. She was still trying to wrap her head around the idea that Emile had called her and asked for her help. She hadn't heard from him, personally, since they went off in different directions after residency. And honestly, she'd never expected to. There were times she'd thought she might run into him at a medical conference, and she'd gone over multiple scenarios in her head about how cool and nonchalant she would play it, all "ha ha, I don't miss you at all."

Of course, it had never happened. He never seemed to attend.

And she really did still miss him. Even after all this time. She'd been so in love with him, even if they'd never said it. It had hurt so much when it all ended.

She'd gotten on with her life, but every once in a while she'd wonder about him. A fleeting thought from a song that they'd danced to, or a joke they'd shared.

It had taken her time to heal, to accept it, but she knew now that they couldn't have been together. He'd made it clear he didn't want a family.

Whereas she did.

Do you, Nuka?

She hadn't actually gone out and made that dream come true, but it was so hard to do when she was so focused on her work.

Saving lives.

Sure. That's the real reason.

She shook that little voice out of her head. Yes, she thought about Emile still, but never expected to see him again.

And then he'd emailed, asking her if he could call, and they talked.

He sounded the same as ever over the phone, but also different.

So formal.

Emile had always been a bit broody, when they'd been working together. The attendings and nurses liked to call them "storm cloud" and "rainbow." Chloé had never minded that, but over the phone his stormy, grumpy personality had seemed a bit grouchier than back then. Not grouchy… Maybe more hermit-like? Crabby?

Great. You're comparing the great love of your life to a crab. Not the best metaphor, Chloé.

Of course, it was not hard to let your mind wander when taking a late-night drive from Ottawa to Montreal.

The suite in the residence hotel that Emile's hospital had set up for her was amazing. It was within walking distance to the hospital, had a gorgeous view of downtown Montreal and the bed was a huge king. Bigger than the bed she had at her sparse apartment in Ottawa, and definitely more luxurious than her lodgings when she stayed in Iqaluit every three months.

Montreal seemed way over-the-top.

Though she tried to get a decent night's sleep in that large bed before her first day at the hospital, she just couldn't. All night she tossed and turned, because she was completely nervous to see Emile again. Which was so silly, right? They had parted ways fairly amicably, even if every time she thought about it, it still felt like a knife had been jabbed into her heart and twisted. Those were just feelings. The facts were they both had wanted very different things and it made sense that they didn't end up together.

She could see that now. It really all made sense.

Nuka, you're being foolish. You loved him.

Immi's words in her head made her smile. Even though they'd been twins, Immitaq had been older by five minutes and liked to rub it in by calling Chloé "little sister."

Immi had been her other half. Now she was Chloé's guiding voice and she missed her fiercely. And even though Immi had never lived to meet Emile, Chloé knew how Immi was a romantic at heart. *You loved him.* That was exactly what she would say to Chloé if she were still alive.

She'd died at sixteen; she'd had so many big dreams she hadn't gotten to live out, but Chloé had done her best to live her own. Maybe Immi would have berated her for not falling in love or having a family by now, but Chloé couldn't help others like her late sister if she wasn't spending her time learning and researching. It was important.

So love and romance took a backseat. She'd find time for it. Eventually. The most important thing was to save as many lives as she could right now. There was no way other families would suffer like hers had when Immi died. Not on her watch.

Chloé knew her sister would have understood.

Sort of.

I'm doing this so others won't lose their loved ones. So others won't lose the Immi in their life. I'm not squandering anything.

As she made her way down the street toward Hôpital de Ville-Marie the next morning, her heart was hammering a steady pound between her ears. All she could think about was not putting her foot in her mouth when she saw Emile again.

I've got to be cool.

The thought made her roll her eyes. That in itself was so not cool. She had nothing to worry about. There were no romantic intentions here. It was all work.

Besides, surely by now, Emile had married some francophone socialite. Whereas, she had stayed married to her job this past decade. Too focused on saving as many lives as she could and bringing more skilled physicians to the north so that no one would have to die needlessly without the proper health care access, just like her twin.

Immi was her whole reason for doing what she did every day. And now as she stared up at the gorgeous hospital where Emile was head of cardio, all she could think about was her twin and what she would say to her right now.

Dang, Nuka, stop standing there. Get a move on you and do your job. Ailiruk eh!

Chloé smiled, lifted her head high and marched right into Hôpital de Ville-Marie like she belonged there, because she did. She was a surgeon and a damn fine surgeon, too. However much she sometimes still felt like that little girl from the north, lost in the big city.

I've got this.

She closed her eyes and took a deep, calming breath. When she opened them, she got her first real look at the modern, open-concept foyer. The glass walls rose high and covered the old brick wall of the original hospital facade. Windows from the seven floors overlooked the space. As she gazed up through the glass roof, she could see white fluffy clouds treading across the blue sky.

"Beautiful, *non*?"

Chloé's pulse skipped a beat because she recognized that voice. She turned around and tried not to gawk at the man she'd been so head over heels in love with a decade ago.

There were some subtle changes to Emile. His jaw was a bit more defined, none of the baby fat of youth. His hair was still that same dark ebony, but with some thick silver strands in the mop of carefully trimmed curls on top. His dark eyes didn't sparkle and there were a few lines on his face, marking the passage of time, but she had to admit she really liked the Van Dyke beard he had going on.

Then she realized she'd been staring too long at him and tried to plaster on the most suave and sophisticated smile she could. And answer him calmly. Professionally.

"Lots of glass. It *shatters* my expectations." And then she winked exaggeratedly, before cringing inwardly at the horrible pun that just slipped past her lips.

Emile's eyes widened slightly, like he was alarmed. He didn't smile. An awkward tension settled between them. Chloé could almost hear the *badum-ting* following the epic failure of that pun.

It's lack of sleep. That's why I'm making bad jokes.

Except, she didn't think that was it at all. She could almost hear Immi groaning at her.

So not cool, Nuka.

"Get it?" she added, desperately, giving Emile a slight nudge in the ribs, hoping it would make it better.

It didn't.

No, Nuka. No.

"I do," Emile agreed, but still didn't smile or acknowledge the humor in any way. "Still a joker, I see. That hasn't changed."

His tone stung, but Chloé couldn't really expect anything less from him. "Still on a serious streak, are we?"

She half expected a comeback or some witty repartee, like they'd shared in the old days.

Instead, Emile's eyes narrowed. "Well, how about we get your identification cards and then we can chat about the case?"

"Sure."

Emile turned and Chloé followed him.

Nuka, easy with the jokes.

She was already off to a great start. If she didn't pull herself together, this whole situation would drag on forever, which was the last thing she wanted. She was half tempted to turn round and run.

Except she couldn't. There was a life on the line.

It was clear Emile had changed, that was all. And that wasn't a problem. This was a working relationship and this Emile, for all intents and purposes, was a stranger.

CHAPTER TWO

EMILE DIDN'T MENTION her epic failure of a pun at all. Actually, he didn't really say much as they walked in awkward silence side by side. He seemed to move through this hospital on autopilot, which wasn't surprising. She knew he'd been working here since they finished their residency in Toronto, and that this was the place his father had worked at before that.

Emile had mentioned enough times that generations of his family had been involved in or worked at Hôpital de Ville-Marie.

In fact, the whole cardiac unit was named after his family. Once they'd gotten all Chloé's identification and passes set up, they made their way over to the Moreau wing, where she could see the line of photographs and plaques, all with Emile's last name etched into the gold plates below.

She couldn't even imagine such a family legacy.

She was the first doctor and surgeon in her family, the first to go to university. Her sister hadn't even been allowed to make it past sixteen.

A pang of guilt washed over Chloé and she swallowed the lump in her throat. Though they'd been twins, she'd never been sick, always healthy, whereas Immi had struggled all her short life.

Life was so unfair.

Walking through the long hall to Emile's office,

Chloé got a kind of creepy feeling that all of Emile's ancestors were watching them, judging them. She couldn't help but wonder if he felt it, too.

If she had to live with that every day, she might be a bit formal as well.

When they'd been interns and then residents together, she'd always felt like he was a bit too hard on himself. A bit of a perfectionist. Now, walking down this hallway to a wing named after his family, she could see why.

"After you, Doctor MacDonald," Emile said, holding open the door to a small meeting room.

"Thank you." Chloé stepped inside.

Emile shut the door, then pulled out a leather high-backed chair for her. She nodded, thanking him again as she sat down and set her computer bag on the floor. Emile took the seat next to her, lacing his fingers together and resting his hands on the table, his back ramrod straight. No expression on his face. No warmth in his eyes.

It made Chloé sad.

"I'm so glad you were able to come and assist me, Doctor MacDonald."

Still with the formality, eh?

"You can call me Chloé. I like to keep it informal."

"It's a bit different here in the city."

Chloé frowned. "I also work in Ottawa, in the capital of Canada, a city. I like to keep it informal and would prefer if you call me Chloé. However,

I can call you Doctor Moreau if that's what you prefer."

Emile's lips pressed together in a firm line and she knew that tight expression meant she was bugging him. That was sort of how their relationship had always played out. Classic grumpy/sunshine. Except this went beyond a mere rain cloud. He was like a massive, pressure-filled storm front.

"Very well, but around patients I would prefer to keep things formal," he agreed grudgingly.

"I can do that." She leaned back, relieved he'd given her that concession. Maybe there was hope for him yet. "I have looked over all your files."

"Good. I expected no less."

She bristled at his tone. "You expected no less? I'm not an intern."

"I know, you're a professional. That's why I didn't doubt you would prepare."

Part of her wanted to scream that it was her, that it was Chloé, and they didn't need this frosty formality! But she swallowed that urge. "Oh. Well, yes. I have gone through what you sent over."

"Is it what I think?"

"Heart cancer?" she asked.

"Oui."

"Then yes. You said you haven't had much experience with heart cancer?"

"No. I haven't. I also don't typically get pediatric patients. I am one of the best cardiothoracic surgeons in the province, though. I have worked on small hearts, but I haven't removed cancer from them. It seems…delicate."

"It is," she replied gently. "I've worked on three patients of this age. Younger even."

A smile crept across Emile's lips then; that twinkle that had been missing a moment ago sparked back to life in his blue eyes. "I know. It's why I reached out. You're talented. But then I've always known that."

No one stood up to Emile. It was refreshing that Chloé did. Frustrating, but he actually didn't mind it.

He was trying to keep a very professional wall up between them, because the moment he'd seen her, he'd realized she hadn't changed at all. It was like time hadn't passed and he was still staring at the same woman he'd fallen for all those years ago. Her dark brown hair was weaved into a long braid that hung down her back. Her luscious lips were painted red and her warm brown eyes were full of awe. He remembered the way her long lashes would brush against his face when they kissed.

The only difference was she now had traditional Inuk tattoos on her fingers.

That was something she had talked about getting done when she finished residency, and he was glad to see she had followed through with that tradition. But then when she said she was going to do something, she usually did it.

Like Emile and his determination to work here

at Hôpital de Ville-Marie. They were similar in that way.

And as much as he wanted to keep that professional wall up, it was hard to do that when he was in her presence, because he remembered all those times they were together. The way they worked together, totally in sync, the fun they had and how much he missed her when it all ended.

Then she'd made that terrible pun.

He'd actually gotten a kick out of it, but couldn't acknowledge it. He didn't want to get too chummy with her. Working together on a case was fine, but having her slowly creep back into his life would not be acceptable. If he started goofing around with her again, then it was a slippery slope indeed.

Yet, it was so easy to forget himself when he was around her. He was already kicking himself for giving her that compliment about her talent. Then again, it was the truth.

Pink tinged Chloé's cheeks and she dipped her head slightly. "Thank you."

"There's no need to thank me, Chloé. Your reputation and work is admirable. I have only seen one heart cancer patient in my time here at Hôpital de Ville-Marie and it was an adult male. Not in a heart tiny like this. I would like to learn, so please keep me informed and include my residents and interns whenever possible. We are a teaching hospital here."

"You want *me* to teach your students? Are you sure?"

He frowned, annoyed that she would doubt herself. "Of course. That is why you're here."

"Well, I'm happy to teach, if you think they can learn from me."

"*Bonne.* So, how do we proceed?"

"Well, there's a few steps we have to take before we can do the surgery." Chloé reached down and pulled out her laptop, opening it. "I find shrinking the tumor with a combination of chemotherapy and radiation is effective. Also, immunotherapy."

"That is a lot to put a child through."

"I understand, but we have to shrink this tumor. It's quite large for someone so young." Chloé sighed. "We have to. It's nowhere else in her body? This is a primary malignant angiosarcoma?"

"*Oui,*" Emile replied. "The CT scans I sent you were the most recent. It's just a very large malignant angiosarcoma in her heart. She presented with back pain, shortness of breath and extreme fatigue. It was during her initial exam that she began to cough up blood and the scans were ordered."

"Poor kid," Chloé murmured. "I would like to see her. I assume she's been admitted?"

"Of course. We can see her right away. Her mother is the premier of the province, and is most anxious to have a plan of attack."

Chloé smiled. "An attack on cancer? I like this mother's way of thinking."

"Well, again, she is premier…"

"I've dealt with my fair share of politicians and I

know how they can be. Especially when it involves something personal to them."

Emile cocked an eyebrow. "Oh?"

Chloé laughed nervously and shook her head as she typed in some notes on her laptop. "Just bureaucratic stuff. Trying to get more surgeons and physicians in the north."

"I'm surprised that you are in Ottawa."

Her eyes narrowed. "What do you mean by that?"

"Well, when we left you were off to Yellowknife. You stayed there for a few months."

"Keeping tabs on me?" she asked slyly.

"Maybe, but I keep tabs on all the residents from our class."

Liar.

"I worked there for a couple of years actually, flying back and forth, before I was offered a place at Ottawa, which meant that I could be put on rotation to work in Iqaluit. Ottawa is closer to Iqaluit than Yellowknife. It's geography, Emile."

"I didn't mean to offend."

Chloé shrugged with indifference. "I understand. I just mean not all of us can stay in the same hospital."

Emile knew it wasn't an insult, but it still stung just the same. There was a part of him, one that existed a long time ago, that wanted to travel and work in different hospitals. The old him regretted giving up that opportunity in Vancouver to come here to Hôpital de Ville-Marie. And then there was another part of him that wished he could go far north, to work in those remote communities like she did. He'd always been fascinated with remote medicine and the north since he was a child.

I did my duty to my father. This is where I belong. I upheld the legacy.

Except, looking at her and all the opportunities she had, the different cases she got to work on… It had certainly given her experience, room to grow, like seeing more heart cancer than he ever did in the city.

"Well, we should go visit the patient and maybe you can request the labs you require and come up with that plan."

This was the part of the job he'd always enjoyed with her, and he could enjoy it again now. He just mustn't let himself get sucked into thinking about the "what-ifs" with her, no matter how tempting it might be.

He was where he was meant to be. Just like she was. All he could hope was that she found happiness there.

"I'm hoping you'll help me, Emile. With the surgery. You say you want to learn. Well, I'll need your skills in the operating room."

Her request caught him off guard. "Of course."

"It's a delicate surgery, and it's complex. It's a team effort and this is your case and your hospital." Chloé smiled warmly, which made his heart skip a beat. She'd always had a way of including him, bringing him joy. It made him want to soften to her, to relax his control…

Keep those walls high, Emile, an inner voice reminded him.

"Of course, I will assist you. It's a rare surgery and a tough case. I would like to learn and assist."

Chloé nodded. "Good."

"I will make sure I get you set up with a workspace and if you need to see patients… I mean, if any of your patients are willing to drive to Montreal to see you then we can give you clinic time."

"No, I was getting ready to do a rotation in Iqaluit. So Montreal is a little far to travel. I might have to disappear for a couple of days to head up to Nunavut, especially if I'm needed, and I might have to head back to Ottawa to see extreme cases."

"Can your patients fly here? Can we transport them here instead of Ottawa?"

Her eyes widened. "I suppose. Would the board of directors be willing to do that? Some of my patients can't afford commercial flights. There's a fund to help in Ottawa…"

"Hôpital de Ville-Marie has a significant fund for that. I'm sure I can speak to the board about allocating some of those funds to accommodate your patients while you are here."

"I would appreciate that."

Their gazes locked and he could feel his wall crumbling again. She had always been able to get under his skin, no matter how serious he was trying to be, and it appeared that time hadn't changed that. He would have to be more careful around her.

Yes, he would be working with her, but he had to remember that her time here was short.

Nothing could happen between them.

They were colleagues and nothing more.

Even if there was part of him that wanted, right in this moment, to have just a *little* bit more.

CHAPTER THREE

EMILE GOT CHLOÉ a space to work and left her to go through some paperwork before she had to meet with the patient and her parents later. Once she was alone, Chloé was able to get herself settled and take a few deep breaths to calm down. She was still in disbelief that she was even here.

Why had she thought this job was going to be easy?

Not the case—heart cancer was never easy—but she really had thought that enough time had passed under the proverbial bridge that she wouldn't be drawn to Emile the same way that she had been before. Instead, even though he was very aloof and closed off, there was a part of her that wanted to try to warm him up, to break past that facade.

She couldn't let herself get sucked into anything with him again. They'd made it clear when they broke up that they were on different paths, wanted different things.

Except, all she had pursued since was medicine. Not a family or a partner, like she'd claimed to want.

How can I have that when there are patients like Immi who need me?

Chloé ignored that little thought. It was clear that the circumstances that had triggered their breakup were still in play and unlikely ever to change. Emile was the head of his department here at Hôpital de Ville-Marie; Chloé never expected him to give that up. And her life wasn't going to change, either—she was happy with her work.

She was exactly where she wanted to be, except for the fact that there could be better health services in the north. At least she was making a difference. She was helping people.

People like Immi.

Just thinking about Immi made her heart twinge. It was a grief she always carried, but never spoke of. It was easier to hide it all, put on that happy face. Her family had been through enough; she didn't want them to have to worry about her, too.

When Emile knocked at her office door, Chloé realized she'd lost an hour to her thoughts, which was so unlike her.

"You all right?" Emile asked as he stepped into her office.

"Why wouldn't I be?"

"Well, we were supposed to meet out in the hallway ten minutes ago."

"Oh?" Chloé glanced at her watch. "Right. I was getting caught up on some work and I didn't sleep the best last night."

It was an excuse and one she hoped he bought.

Emile cocked an eyebrow. "Was the room not to your liking? The hotel is one of the best residence short-stay hotels in this area."

"No, it's not that. The room was fine. It's just..." She trailed off. When they were residents, she would have said that she could talk to him about anything. But had that been true? She hadn't told him everything about her life. She'd never talked about Immitaq and she knew there were things Emile had never told her.

It was something she had often wondered about after their breakup. Had they really known each other at all, or had it merely been just physical attraction and the stress of the residency that brought them together?

Still, he was someone she could usually confide in about work, at least. But right now she felt something holding her back.

"It's just what?" Emile asked softly, the formality slipping just a bit.

As their gazes locked, for one brief moment, Chloé could see the Emile whom she had fallen for all those years ago; the Emile who loved surgery and wanted to make a difference. It was like he was still hiding there under the surface.

Then the moment passed, and he was gone. This was not that Emile, not the one she thought she knew. There was no intimacy there. No trust. He was a stranger with a familiar face.

She wasn't going to talk to him about Immi or the fact that she still felt that troubling pull of attraction toward him. He didn't need to know those things. All she had to talk to him about was the case.

That was it.

"I have a lot on my mind. My own patients back

in Ottawa and in Iqaluit. Now this young child with heart cancer."

They were colleagues and nothing more and she'd have to keep reminding herself of that fact. And it was true; she was thinking about her patients and this child whom she was here to see.

Work was her life.

It always had been.

There hadn't been time for dating or really a social life. All her focus had been on her career; her energy and her drive completely centered around that, so that no one would have to lose a family member the way she had. She had a life. Immitaq didn't. Chloé had to use the time she'd been given for good.

"I've been thinking a lot about this case, too," Emile said. "I find it vastly frustrating that a child has cancer and that I cannot solve the issue on my own."

"Heart cancer is rare. Especially primary angiosarcoma in a pediatric patient. Don't beat yourself up over the fact you haven't worked on enough cases. Be thankful you haven't."

Their eyes met again, and again for a second she could see the empathy, the pain, the drive to eradicate this disease in him. Warmth spread through her and she smiled. It was that passion for medicine that had brought them together all those years ago.

His lips pursed together in a thin line and he tore his gaze away, the brief spell broken once more. "Well, when you put it that way, I suppose you are right. Still, I don't want to let any patient down. There is a reason they come here to Hôpital de Ville-Marie and not somewhere else. We are the best here."

"No doubt." Chloé mustered a fake smile, because she wasn't sure what else there was to say to that. The boast annoyed her. He wasn't wrong; his hospital did have that reputation, but they'd had to bring her in to help. The way he'd always placed this hospital on a pedestal even in their days in residency was one of the reasons they broke up. There had only ever been one path for Emile.

She'd kept an eye on his work, too, over the years, and Emile was just as talented as she was and had achieved everything he'd wanted. If he'd been pigeonholed here at Hôpital de Ville-Marie, then he'd been the one taking every step possible to make it happen. So why did she get the feeling that he wasn't actually happy about it? Like what he'd achieved still wasn't enough.

He'd always been chasing something here, something more than the department head role. Chloé just didn't know what.

It's not my concern.

"Well, we better go and meet with the patient and her parents."

"Yes. Let's do that." Chloé stood up and followed Emile out of her office.

They didn't say anything to each other as they made their way down to the pediatric wing of the cardiothoracic unit. The hallways were brightly colored; there were beautiful sunflowers and other happy paintings on the walls, but as Chloé glanced through windows, the sight of tiny bodies in the beds or walking the floor made her stomach twist in a knot.

In those little faces, all she could see was Immi.

It was the same whenever she saw sick children. And it was why she always worked doubly hard when it came to the youngest patients.

"Right here," Emile said, stopping and opening the door.

She nodded quickly and followed him into the room. Emile began speaking rapid French but she could follow most of it.

A woman with dark circles under her eyes stood up, extending her hand. "It's a pleasure to meet you, Doctor MacDonald. I'm Agathe Paquette and this is my husband, Tomas."

Tomas just nodded and didn't get up from where he was sitting at his daughter's bedside.

"A pleasure to meet you," Chloé greeted, but she couldn't take her eyes off the tiny girl, so little in that big bed. Her face was sunken and she was hooked up to far too many monitors for someone who was six.

"This is my daughter, Céline," Agathe introduced. "Céline, this is Doctor MacDonald."

Céline's gaze latched on to hers. Chloé could see immediately that she was wary of doctors and being poked and prodded.

"You can call me Chloé," she said.

Céline smiled slightly. "I like your earrings."

Chloé reached up and touched the beaded earrings she was wearing. Immitaq had made them for her, but she couldn't bring her sister up in this room or she might cry. "They were a gift. I got them a long time ago."

"They're pretty." Céline coughed; it sounded a bit raspy, like even the mere act of a small cough was too much exertion for the child.

"Do you mind if I listen to your heart?" Chloé grabbed the stethoscope that was lying on the table with some other medical instruments.

"Sure," Céline consented.

Chloé smiled and then sat down gently on the edge of the bed while Tomas helped his daughter to sit up. She could see on the monitors that the vitals weren't great and as she listened to her breathing and heart, it was clear that Céline's heart was failing.

Way too young.

"Thank you, Céline," Chloé responded and helped her lie back down. "I'm going to talk to your mom and dad and then they'll be right back."

"Okay," Céline said.

Chloé stepped out into the hallway with Emile, Agathe and Tomas.

"So," Agathe said as the door closed, "what is the plan?"

"I would like to get another scan with contrast. I want to see if the tumor has grown in the last couple of days."

"You think it could have grown?" Agathe asked, her breath catching in her throat.

"It's a rare cancer," Chloé explained gently. "And before I make my plan, I want to be sure. I would like to shrink it with chemotherapy and do immunotherapy on her before I operate. I want her to be as strong as possible."

Agathe looked at Emile, which Chloé could have been insulted by, but it wasn't surprising. They trusted Emile. He was their doctor and she was the stranger here.

"It's a good plan," Emile agreed.

Agathe nodded. "Do what you can, Doctors."

"We will," Emile assured gently. He may be standoffish with Chloé, but she was pleased to see he was still caring with his patients.

Agathe and Tomas headed back into Céline's room.

"When do you want the scan done?" Emile asked, turning to her and getting straight to business.

"As soon as possible."

Emile nodded. "We can make that happen."

"Good. Once I have that, I'll know the proper dosages to order chemotherapy from your pediatric oncology team here."

"*Bonne*," Emile stated. He looked at his watch. "It's almost lunchtime."

"Do you keep on a schedule?"

He cocked an eyebrow. "I try, but I meant that you might have to wait for a scan. Radiology does close for an hour, unless a trauma case comes in through the emergency room."

"Ah. Right. Lunch. Where can one get a bite to eat around here?"

"There is a cafeteria. Or you could walk to a nearby bistro."

"That sounds like fun! Care to join me?" The invitation came out before she could stop it.

Emile took a step back from her. "Why?"

"To eat?" she asked carefully. "You do eat, yes?"

"I do. Alone usually."

"Well, why don't you eat with me?"

Nuka, what are you doing?

Say no.

Only, Emile didn't. Couldn't. "Very well." He cleared his throat. "I think we have some more things to discuss, after all."

Chloé's eyes widened. "Do we?"

"About the case." What had come over him? He never went out to lunch with anyone. Actually, he never really took a lunch break at all. He would eat something at his desk. So he wasn't sure what compelled him to say yes to a lunch outside the hospital, with Chloé of all people. It must just have been habit, because when they'd been residents they always ate together.

"Great," Chloé said. "I wouldn't mind trying something local to this area of Montreal. It's my first time here."

"This is your first time in Montreal?" he asked, surprised.

"Yes. I've been mostly everywhere else in Canada, but haven't had the pleasure of visiting Quebec. I don't come to the east coast much."

"We're not part of the maritimes."

"I know. I'm just saying that I'm either north or out west but…anyway, yes, let's do lunch out to discuss the case. With you. In case I didn't make that clear."

He tried not to smile. It was hard not to when she was rambling. He'd always thought she was so cute when she was flustered. "You did. How about we meet downstairs in the main foyer in about thirty minutes? That way you have time to set up the testing. Just don't be surprised if they don't get to it right away."

"Good. It's a date." Pink bloomed in her cheeks. "I mean…lunch. Business lunch."

"*Bonne.*" Emile turned on his heel and left, quickly, putting some distance between them. He wasn't going to change his mind about lunch, but he was annoyed that he agreed to the invite anyway.

Falling back into old habits, letting himself be enchanted by her quirks again…

This was not how to maintain a working relationship.

This was not keeping his distance.

CHAPTER FOUR

THERE WERE A few times over the next thirty minutes that Emile considered coming up with some sort of excuse not to go out to lunch with Chloé. Unfortunately, every story he could think of was absolutely ridiculous.

Which made him feel a bit foolish. And irked.

His father had never stood for half-truths or lies and Emile couldn't stand them, either, so the temptation to hide behind one now was frustrating him all the more.

In the end, there was no getting out of it. He'd accepted her invitation and he had to go.

I have a lot of work. I could tell her that.

He always had a lot of work. Usually, he would eat by himself, because that was the way he liked it. He preferred to keep to himself for the most part.

This is why you don't have much of a life, a little voice reminded him. *This can be just business.*

He'd taken other people out for a meal before. This wasn't a foreign notion. He'd wined and dined board members, VIP guests, prestigious donors, so why was this so different?

Annoyed with himself and his thoughts, Emile stood up and pulled off his white lab coat, then grabbed his suede bomber jacket from where it hung on the back of his office door, so that he could leave before he went through another cycle of self-deprecation, trying to convince himself to change his mind.

Again.

Even though Chloé and he had agreed to meet in the foyer, he headed straight for her office where he found her just leaving.

"You ready?" he asked.

Chloé startled, then spun around. "I thought we were meeting downstairs?"

"We were, but I decided to pass by to see if I met up with you." What he didn't tell her was that he'd taken this route so he wouldn't have time to talk himself out of going to lunch with her. He was facing his trepidation head-on.

Her eyes widened. "Oh."

Emile got the distinct impression that she wasn't thrilled by his catching her leaving. Maybe she was having second thoughts about asking him and had been planning to sneak away?

"Oh?" he asked, slightly amused. "Were you going to run out on me and then send me a text, feeding me some excuse?"

That was exactly what he'd thought about, too, but there was no way he was going to tell her that.

"No!" Except Chloé wouldn't look him in the eyes and there was a blush on her cheeks.

Busted.

He chuckled. "You were always a bad liar."

"How so?"

"Remember the time you were late to rounds and

you came up with that ridiculous excuse about the squirrel on the subway?"

She smiled and rolled her eyes, tossing her hair over her shoulders. "Fine. I was going to text you my regrets."

"What did the text say?" he asked, enjoying seeing her squirm.

"It doesn't matter."

"It most definitely does."

Chloé pursed her lips together in an adorable expression of playful frustration. "You're a pain."

"And you are stubborn."

"How am I stubborn?"

"You just won't admit that you were going to cancel on me." He grinned, smugly pleased with himself.

Chloé pulled her phone out of her purse. "Fine. You were right. Happy?"

He leaned over to read the half-typed text. "Very, though I'm disappointed there was no squirrel involved."

"There really was a squirrel on the subway car and it was a menace!"

They both laughed and he felt himself relax. He couldn't remember the last time he'd actually done that; the last time he'd laughed and joked with someone. It had probably been with Chloé. She always had a way of making him feel at ease. It felt nice to be smiling with her again, just like old times.

Unlike old times, though, he had to remember that they were colleagues only. Nothing more. He couldn't let his guard down. As much as he wouldn't mind falling back into bad habits around her, it wouldn't be fair to Chloé.

Their lives were so vastly different. Even if they appeared the same on the surface.

She wanted things he just couldn't commit to giving her. Like children. And time.

"So do you still want to get out of this lunch?" he asked solemnly.

"No. I'm an adult. A professional, and a VIP here. I think the head of the department *should* take me out to lunch." She nodded for effect, mock-serious.

She was so adorable.

Time apart hadn't changed that.

Don't think about her like that. I can't think about her like that.

That sort of thinking would lead him down a very slippery slope, with no possibility of a positive outcome. Nothing had changed about their lives. He wasn't going to hold her back by keeping her here, and he couldn't leave this place.

Why not?

Emile ignored that little voice, the small one inside that made him think about other paths, ones he hadn't taken. "I believe *you* invited *me* out."

"I did, but that was only because you weren't polite enough to offer. After all, I am a guest."

He rolled his eyes. "Indeed. Let's go."

There was no backing out now. They were going out for lunch, even if both of them in their own ways had tried to get out of it. The only difference was that Chloé didn't know that he'd been grappling with his own indecision, and it was going to stay that way.

When they stepped outside, the sun was shining and it was warm.

June was one of Emile's favorite months in Montreal. Warm, but not too warm or humid like the summers could get. The leaves were on the trees and flowers were blooming. It wasn't officially summer yet, still spring, but it felt like a summer's day.

Chloé sighed and closed her eyes, smiling brightly, just like a sunbeam. "Don't you love it?"

"What?" he asked.

"The sun on your face."

Emile shrugged. "I suppose. I mean, it's a nice day…"

She looked at him with exasperation. "Still so enthused, I see."

"What do you mean?"

"It's beautiful out."

He shrugged. "I suppose. It's a typical June day."

"Still can't see the bright side, eh?" she teased.

"And you're still all super sunshine."

Chloé smiled. "And why not?"

He sighed, because he didn't really have much of an answer. How could he have that upbeat attitude when he'd always been forced to hide any sign of emotion? His whole life, he'd had to be serious.

Get good grades.

Be the best.

Become a surgeon. A heart surgeon.

Marry the right person.

Uphold the family name.

That was the course of his life as laid out by his father. Those were the tenets he followed, because if he did, then his father would praise him and see that he was worthy of his name. The only place he'd fallen down was marriage; he refused to marry or have children if his workload meant he'd just have to ignore them.

The family name would die out with him.

Just thinking about his father made a dark cloud settle over him.

"The bistro isn't far from here. Just a short walk," he said, gruffly trying to change the subject as he headed off down the street toward the little restaurant he had in mind. It had a small rooftop patio where they could sit outside and maybe catch a glimpse of the river.

"Sounds good," Chloé replied. "Lead the way, MacDuff."

Emile cocked his head and looked at her quizzically as they walked. "That's not the quote."

Chloé rolled her eyes. "I know, but it's what my father always said when we were out on the land and he wanted me to lead the way. He was teaching me how to navigate out on the tundra in the snow."

"Ah, I see. Well, as long as you know the actual quote from the cursed play."

She grinned. "I took a lot of English literature in my undergrad. The actual quote is 'Lay on,

MacDuff,' but has been reinterpreted to *lead on*, which is what my father would often say to us."

Her expression changed then, just a brief flicker of what looked like regret and pain.

"Us? I thought you were an only child?"

"Slip of the tongue," she replied quickly.

There was a part of Emile that wanted to pry, learn more about her family, her childhood. But if he did that then he'd be opening himself up to her again. He had to keep this a working partnership. Once this surgery was done, she was going back to Ottawa. Montreal was not her home.

They didn't say much else during the short walk to the bistro. The waitress took them to the upstairs rooftop patio, to a small wrought iron table with an umbrella at the far corner. Ivy crept up the old stone walls and they could see a glimpse of the St. Lawrence through the tall modern buildings that dominated the Montreal skyline.

"Gorgeous," Chloé sighed, leaning back in her chair. "I do love how old and modern meet here."

"*Oui.* I do, too. It's *tres bon.* If you really like the old, then you should take a trip to Quebec City. The Chateau Frontenac poised on the cliffs about the old city is formidable."

"I might have to make a weekend getaway there. Anywhere else I should see?"

"The *chutes de Montmorency* and *Sainte Anne de Beaupré.*"

Chloé made a face. "Might have to think on the church, given the history."

"Of course. My apologies for not thinking about that."

"It's okay. I did ask about sightseeing, and I have heard of that church before. So *chutes de Montmorency* is a waterfall, yes?"

He smiled. "*Oui.*"

"I do remember some of my French. Like *tabarnak*!"

Emile's eyes widened. "Don't shout that around here. That's a terrible word. You're cursing."

"Really?" Her eyebrows shot up, then knit into a frown. "I'm going to murder Jerry Aglook if I ever run into him again," she growled. "He taught me that in grade six."

"And what did you think it meant?"

"Tabernacle. Like a building."

Emile smiled slightly. "Well, technically, that's what it means, so Jerry Aglook is not wrong. It's just one of the worst *sacres* or swear words used in Quebec. So, maybe try to keep that word to yourself?"

"Noted."

The waitress approached their table. "*Bonjour et bienvenue!* What can I get for you today?"

"I'll have smoked meat on rye and espresso," he ordered.

"I'll have the same," Chloé replied.

The waitress nodded and took their menus, before disappearing again. A silence descended between them and Emile just stared at Chloé, sitting across from him in the sun. She was still as breathtaking as ever. She always was so hard to resist.

"So," he said, leaning over, "now you know a cuss word in Quebecois, you need to tell me one commonly heard in the north."

Their gazes locked, her eyes widening in surprise. "We don't really have swear words."

"I find that hard to believe."

"Believe it! I suppose you could use the word *huqutaunngittuq*, which means terrible and basically is used to indicate a good-for-nothing." Chloé laughed to herself.

"What?"

"Well, here we are, two surgeons at a business lunch talking about swear words instead of the case. I find it funny."

Her comment reminded him how easy it was for him to forget himself, to let down his walls around her. He couldn't do that, no matter how good it felt.

It had nearly broken him all those years ago when their relationship had ended. He wouldn't hurt himself again that way, and he wouldn't hurt her by starting anything when he knew he couldn't give her what she really wanted. The last thing he wanted to do was cause her pain.

"You're right. We should talk about the case."

Chloé shrugged. "Well, there's not a whole lot to discuss. Not until I have the results of those scans. Once I know if the tumor has grown, then I will know how to proceed."

"Then why did you ask me out to lunch?"

Pink tinged her cheeks. "Habit, I suppose."

"I could be working." Instead of sitting here and being tempted by her.

She sat up a little straighter, tapping her hands against the table. "You're right. We need to talk about the case. It's a business lunch, so yes, let's draw up some battle plans."

He felt bad for calling her out, so he smiled at her to soften the criticism. "Like Macbeth calling into MacDuff to fight? Lay on, MacDuff."

She nodded. "Exactly."

There were some other words in Inukitut Chloé could've taught Emile, but again, they weren't really curse words in the way he meant. It was more about how one used a word, contextually, that could make it an insult. Like the way she often called him an *aiviq* or a walrus in her head whenever she thought about their breakup years ago.

Then again, that wasn't really fair to walruses in general, because she liked them. They didn't deserve to get caught up in the mess between her and Emile.

Still, it was funny how, after the awkward silence that had fallen on them as they'd walked from the hospital to the bistro, the moment they'd sat down at their table it had been as though no time had passed at all. It had felt like they were those two silly residents in Toronto again.

In truth, she'd forgotten about the squirrel incident.

There was a lot that she'd tried to put out of her

mind when they'd broken up. It was just easier on her heart that way. Pain was something she'd learned to easily hide. It was good to mask the pain and just keep it to herself, instead of burdening others.

And as much as she didn't want to let Emile in, it was so hard to remember the walls she'd built to keep him out, because he was so easy to talk to and he always had been.

"Chere, you should be studying," he whispered in her ear as they sat on the couch of her tiny little apartment, his arm draped over her shoulder and his breath on her neck. Studying was not what she was thinking about and it was clear that wasn't on his mind, either.

"Oh? And what are you doing? I thought we were going to watch this surgical procedure on the television. I mean, it's studying an important surgical technique."

He sat up straighter. "Then why do you have popcorn? I assumed you were going to put on a movie."

"Well, it's a surgery movie type of thing."

He looked at her curiously. "You eat popcorn and watch surgeries?"

"Not live." She grinned and then picked up the remote. "What movie were you thinking of?"

"I don't care." He smiled lazily and then ran his finger down her neck.

"Right, so why are you pestering me about studying when all you want to do is make out to a bad movie?"

"Well, studying anatomy is important," he teased, his voice low and husky.

"Is it?" Her pulse began to race. "I thought you aced anatomy in medical school?"

"I did." He kissed her then, tantalizingly slow, making her melt. "I could use a refresher. How about you?"

Chloé's cheeks heated and she tried to chase away that memory of him, of their impromptu anatomy class on her couch that was probably the best she'd ever attended.

The one she'd taken in medical school had involved a lot of heaving and gagging as people couldn't stand the sight of their first cadaver.

Chloé, though, had stood the test.

She'd had to, because there was no way she could let her average drop, lose her scholarship to the Northern Ontario Medical School at Lakehead and have to go back home having failed her family. Having failed Immitaq.

"You okay?" Emile asked, intruding on her thoughts.

"Yep. Why?"

"You zoned out there."

"Just…thinking." Which was true. Thinking about his kisses, the way he made her feel safe, how much it had hurt when things ended.

It had been for the best.

Was it?

"About the rate of immunotherapy?" he asked.

Huh?

"Yep. Totally."

He looked at her dubiously. Before she had to explain herself further, the waitress returned then with their food. The steaming smoked meat was piled high on the marbled rye. The scent made her stomach growl with complete appreciation. She'd had smoked meat before, in a deli in Toronto, but she knew Montreal was the home of the spiced treat, and she couldn't wait to sink her teeth into it.

"*Bon appétit*," the waitress said.

"*Merci*," Chloé responded. The waitress left and she picked up her sandwich, savoring that first bite. "So good."

"It is the best," Emile agreed.

"Tomorrow I want a bagel. And then I want poutine and then tortiere."

He chuckled. "You're making quite the list for Quebec."

"You know it. I'm not here for a fun reason, but I'm going to also enjoy my time here." She took a sip and looked out across the city. "Maybe I'll take the train to Quebec City, so I can enjoy the ride along the river."

"You could… Or I can drive you."

The offer, though it sounded a bit forced, made her heart skip a beat. "What?"

"There is a bookstore I like to frequent in the old city, so I don't mind going with you to show you around. I mean…we can be friends, right?"

Startled, she said, "I would like that. Friends is good."

It was true; she would like it. She just wasn't sure they could do it. They'd tried to be friends before, but that turned into friends with benefits, which then turned into something more and then, ultimately heartache.

She didn't think she could survive another heartbreak with Emile. So if they were going to try out this friend thing, which she was highly suspicious of, she'd have to be careful.

"*Bonne.* Then, before you leave, we'll plan a weekend to go to Quebec City and the falls, but no church." He took a sip of his coffee. "Hopefully, it will be soon."

"You want me to leave that fast, eh?" It was just a tease; she knew he was being optimistic about Céline's case.

"No, but...you know why."

"I do. I want to win this for Céline, too. No parent should have to lose their child." Chloé only hoped her voice didn't catch in her throat.

She could hear her mother sobbing from her bedroom. Her now-empty bedroom. Not completely empty. She was still there, but there was a hole, a space that still belonged to Immitaq, and it felt like this great chasm in her heart.

"I have to be strong for anaana and ataata. I have to be brave for them. Strong for them. They need me."

No one had been there to be strong for her. Now she was here, to be strong for those who couldn't be. It was the least she could do. Why else had she survived?

Every life she saved was an Immitaq saved for a loved one, so that person didn't have to experience that pain and that grief her parents had felt.

The excruciating pain Chloé had felt, and still felt to this day.

Both of them sat in silence, eating their smoked meat sandwiches and staring out over the city. She was trying to formulate the right words to continue a lighthearted conversation and keep the emotion of Immi from leaking out.

Her phone buzzed, notifying her of an email. When she picked it up, she could see that it was from the radiologist.

"Well?" Emile asked.

"It's from Doctor Garneau and it's the results of Céline's scans. I guess they worked through lunch."

"I'm glad they did. What does Doctor Garneau say?"

"I'm reading," she mumbled as she read through the report and then opened it up. The images were small on her phone screen; she'd analyze them more closely when she got back to her office. But the report told her everything she needed to know and it was hard to control her expression in the face of such disheartening news.

She knew that Emile would know instantly what was in that email, and his stony tone confirmed it. "Tell me."

"The tumor has grown. It's rapidly progressing."

"I see."

"I know how to attack this. When we get back, I'll order the correct protocol and we'll get her on some strong chemotherapy and radiation to stop the growth and shrink the tumor before we operate."

Emile frowned. “Aggressive. It sounds so wrong for a small child.”

“It is, but the good news in all of this is it hasn’t spread. Of course, it’s just a matter of time before it does, but in all honesty, with the rate the tumor is increasing in her heart, it will kill her before it metastasizes anywhere else.”

“How about I pay this bill and we head back—if you’re done, that is?”

“I’m done. And I did invite you out. I can pay.”

“No,” Emile stated. “The hospital will.”

“Okay, thanks. I want to get back, too, and start the protocol. This whole process is just going to be a bit of hurry-up-and-wait for the foreseeable future.”

Emile nodded and headed downstairs to the main part of the bistro. Chloé finished the last bite of her sandwich and chugged her espresso, staring at the bleak images one last time. There was a part of her that had been hoping the tumor hadn’t grown and that the course of treatment wouldn’t be as complex. Not only because it would be better for Céline, but also, selfishly, because then Chloé wouldn’t have had to remain so long in Montreal, putting her own heart in danger. Instead, it was looking like Montreal was going to be her home for some time.

But all that really didn’t matter in the grand scheme of things. All that mattered was making sure that little Céline came through this, so that she had a chance to grow up and live a normal life.

Chloé’s heart could handle the threat.

For now.

CHAPTER FIVE

THEY WALKED BACK to the hospital in silence. Something had shifted since Dr. Garneau sent over that report. There had been a few moments during lunch where she saw snippets of the Emile she remembered, but when reality had hit and those scans came through, his demeanor had changed.

It was like all that old familiarity had been left back at the bistro. Chloé was trying to chalk it up to the urgency of the situation.

"Would you like to come to my office and we can review the scans there?" she asked as they stepped back into the atrium of the hospital.

"No. I have too much to do." Emile barely looked at her. "I shouldn't have gone out."

The last sentence was a bit of a mumble that caught her off guard.

"For lunch?" she asked quizzically.

He frowned. "I am the chief of cardiothoracic. Again, my time is limited. I should've been at my desk when the scans came in."

"They were sent to me."

He wasn't looking at her, but checking his phone. "Send me your report."

"I thought you want to learn?" Chloé asked. "This is a hands-on moment." An increase in professionalism was one thing, but this total shift in his personality had her stunned.

"I do. I can read and learn as well."

Before she could argue any further, he quickly walked away.

She rolled her eyes and headed back to her office. He was acting a bit like his father. She'd only met Dr. Moreau Senior once, when he came to the hospital in Toronto. She hadn't liked the energy he put out then, and had been glad Emile was so different. Now, though, it felt like he was trying to be like his late father.

It wasn't her concern, though. Emile could act however he wanted. As long as it didn't interfere with his work.

When she got back to her office space, she pulled the images up on her computer to study them. It had been one thing seeing the images on her phone and reading Dr. Garneau's report. It was another thing entirely to see the tumor on a larger screen and realize what a fight it was going to be. There was going to be a *lot* of medication for Céline to handle.

Carefully, she started to put together the plan of attack to present to Céline's parents. Just from her brief meeting with Céline's mother, she knew that Agathe was going to want all the facts—not that she would do less for any of her patients.

She wanted all them to have every option available. Especially the littlest and most precious ones like Céline.

Chloé's parents hadn't always been in the know

about Immi's diagnosis and they had cycled through an endless revolving door of doctors, depending on who was doing their rotation up north that month.

"But we were told the stage of heart failure wasn't so bad," her mother said softly, completely confused.

"Who told you that?" the new doctor asked.

"Doctor Gerrity," her father answered.

The new doctor scoffed. "Well, no offense to Doctor Gerrity, but I'm a heart specialist."

Chloé wandered away from her parents and down to her sister's room. Immi was lying in bed, oxygen cannula in her nose, her little beading loom on her lap. She looked exhausted, just from the act of living.

"What're you making?" Chloé asked.

"Earrings," Immi gasped. "For you."

Chloé smiled. "They're pretty."

"Thanks. I want you to wear them. Always."

Chloé reached up and touched her earrings now. Céline had liked her earrings. Maybe Chloé could make some for her. She often did that for her pediatric patients.

Céline was lucky to be in Montreal, and Chloé was thankful that Emile's hospital was going to allow her patients to come here, too.

It was a kind gesture.

Proof that he could still be kind, even though he was keeping Chloé at an arm's length. No matter how cold he was to her, she could still see the remnants of the man she fell in love with years ago.

There was an empathy that was still lurking under that aloof exterior. It was almost as if this hospital, this place, was weighing him down.

It wasn't so much Montreal; she had been able to see the love he had for the city when they'd gone out for lunch and eaten on that beautiful ivy-covered terrace. So if it wasn't that, then it must be this hospital.

Which seemed odd, given how this had always been the plan for him. Always the endgame.

"But why your late father's hospital? He's no longer there. You can go anywhere," she said. She could tell how sad he was about turning down Vancouver.

Emile frowned. "It's a legacy."

"Ah, legacy shemgacy," she joked, trying to make light of it. Clearly, this was the wrong thing to do. His face hardened.

"And look who is talking," he snapped. "You're going to go to Iqaluit. That plan hasn't changed. What is so different about my plans compared to yours?"

Emile had had a point. And now Chloé couldn't help thinking of that painting of his father and all the others that had come before him, glaring down at him… She couldn't even begin to imagine that kind of pressure. She also knew that Emile was stubborn and wouldn't walk away from something he had worked so hard to achieve.

Why should you worry?

The answer was simple. She shouldn't. They were

colleagues, friends, that was it. They weren't lovers, and given the way their lives were going and the fact that they lived in completely different worlds, she didn't really see them ever getting back together. Ever.

Even if Emile was still as dishy and tempting as he'd been all those years ago when they'd first met. The same smile, the same laugh, that made her feel so comfortable—when he let her see them. When he was himself. The closed-off workaholic he'd become, she wasn't too keen on. If she ever decided to get married and have kids, she wanted an equal partner. Someone who could be there; someone to rely and lean on.

Emile was not that person.

And no amount of desire or wishing would change that.

Chloé groaned in frustration and ran her fingers through her hair.

What she needed to do now was focus.

"Come on. You can do this," she grumbled to herself as she stared at her report.

"Do what?"

Chloé glanced up to see the very man who was distracting her from her work, hovering in the door to her office.

"Work," she replied and then sat up straighter. "What're you doing here?"

Emile sighed. "I came to apologize. I got…distracted. I like to be here when news like that comes in. Also, it's been about an hour since we came back, so I'm looking for the report."

Chloé leaned back in her chair, crossing her arms. "I was just going to send you my report."

"I appreciate it, but I'm here now."

"Well, then by all means, come on in." She pulled up the images, mumbling about finicky behavior.

"What?" he asked.

"Nothing. Just muttering to myself." She smiled, glad he hadn't heard her complaints.

"I'd forgotten you talk to yourself."

"I don't do it that often!"

Emile smiled, his blue eyes twinkling briefly. "You do. You have full conversations with yourself. And you talk in your sleep."

Heat bloomed in her cheeks. "Well, I can't confirm or deny that…"

"I assure you, you do. 'Kill the elves' was my favorite of your nocturnal shouting matches. It scared me half to death when you sat upright in bed, screamed that and went back to sleep. I always did mean to ask what you were dreaming about that night."

Chloé groaned. "Can I help you with anything *medical*, Doctor Moreau, or is this visit merely to discuss my unconscious effort to go marauding on innocent fay folk? I honestly don't know if I'm coming or going with you."

He looked away, shoving his hands in his coat pockets like he was a bit on edge. His lips pressed together in a firm line. "I'm aware. My apologies. I keep to myself mostly."

"People who want to be friends usually are a bit more social."

"I'm out of practice," he admitted.

"Indeed. Well, you're forgiven. Now, tell me what you think of these scans."

Emile leaned over her, close. She closed her eyes, drinking in the scent of him; she always did love the way he smelled.

Nuka, seriously?

"That is a nasty tumor," Emile remarked.

"It is."

They shared a look. Chloé realized her pulse was racing. Then Emile abruptly stood up, taking a step back like he was pushing her away. "You have a course of action?" he asked.

"Working on it."

Emile nodded. "Good."

She thought that was going to be the end of it, but he lingered.

"You know, I can't think with people hovering over me," Chloé teased. "Something else is on your mind."

"Indeed. You know, I have a very unique ventricular septal defect repair in about an hour, and I was hoping you'd like to join me."

Chloé was definitely intrigued by the prospect. A VSD repair was a simple enough procedure and she'd done the operation herself countless times, but the fact that Emile said it was unusual had her interested.

“What makes it so special?” she asked, curious.

“Well, the patients are conjoined twins. This is the first step in determining their eventual separation. One of the twins has a ventricular septal defect and in order to get them strong enough to be separated, both their hearts need to be strong.”

“Conjoined twins?” It was true; that was very rare. She hadn’t seen many cases in the north at all. Well, not in her jurisdiction. And she was very tempted. He might be learning from her about heart cancer, but this was an opportunity for her to learn from him.

“Well, are you interested in joining me in the operating room?”

“Yes. I would like that. Thank you for asking me. You’re right—I don’t get a lot of cases like that in Ottawa or in Iqaluit.”

“Good. The procedure is in an hour and in operating room four. I’ll meet you down there.”

“Yes.”

Emile nodded and slipped out of her office just as quietly as he entered. She was so thankful for the opportunity, but there was a part of her that was a bit concerned about where this could go. She’d fallen in love with him the last time over surgery, the way they’d always worked together so seamlessly in the operating room. Sure, they bantered outside, but it was in that moment of surgery, staring at a heart, when it had felt like they were truly one.

There was a deep connection. Wouldn't this be just setting herself up for something similar? Put her in danger of falling for him again?

Not if I don't let it.

She would only be observing, really. A VSD didn't require many hands. Besides, Emile would be right there with her when they did Céline's surgery. This would be a good test of her willpower.

Emile had sent over the file, so Chloé had a chance to look at it all before she headed down to the operating room.

The conjoined twins were connected by liver and bowels. They both had separate hearts, but there were parts where they shared a blood supply. Twin A's heart had the VSD and that hole in the heart was affecting the blood supply to Twin B. So before they could be separated, Twin A had to have their ventricular septal defect repaired. And then when it was safe, the separation surgery would occur. Chloé wished she'd be around then to watch or lend a hand, but that was at least a year away, maybe more. Conjoined twins were never separated surgically until they were at least a year old.

She wouldn't be here then.

Montreal was not her endgame.

Maybe she'd be able to come back and watch it?

Do you think that's a good idea? Immi's voice questioned.

It probably wasn't.

She got a pair of scrubs, changing quickly in

the locker room, tying back her hair under a generic scrub cap—she'd left her personalized ones in Ottawa—then she headed into the scrub room to wash and get masked up. As she scrubbed in, she could see Emile was already in the operating room and she paused for a moment to admire him. She'd forgotten how good he looked in his dark blue scrubs.

Sometimes, back when they were residents, she'd stand in the gallery to watch him work, mesmerized by his focus and trying not to think about the fact she knew exactly what was under those scrubs.

Her face heated under her mask, thinking about a few times when things had gotten hot and heavy in the on-call room.

Oh, my God. I'm doing it again.

Friends don't usually lust after one another, Nuka, Immi's voice reminded her.

Chloé groaned quietly under her breath and shook off her hands before stepping into the operating room to get gloved and gowned by one of the OR nurses. The moment she stepped into that room, she just shut out all those thoughts about Emile and the past and focused on the surgery and this amazing opportunity to see a complex VSD repair.

The operating room was a calming place for her, where she was able to just focus on her work and clear her mind. As she approached the table, though, she had to look twice to take in the sight of the two tiny babies, joined together and hooked up to so many lines and monitors. There were scans and fluoroscopy imaging on the screens around the room so they could see how the blood was moving through the arteries, the structure of Twin A's heart and the ventricular septal defect. And just by looking at the twins on the table she could see that Twin A was the more robust of the two.

This repair would definitely make Twin B stronger and more able to withstand the eventual separation when the twins were older.

"What do you think?" Emile asked, coming to stand beside her.

"Twin A is larger," Chloé remarked. "Not knowing all the facts, I can only surmise the situation from your notes, but I think it should be a simple enough repair, even though it's a large VSD. I assume you're doing open chest?"

Emile nodded. "That is the only way to ensure that it will be successful and beneficial for both twins in the long run."

"What're their names?" She hated thinking of them so clinically as Twins A and B. Sometimes it was better to compartmentalize things, but she found she worked better if she formed a connection with her patients, if she knew them.

Even if things went badly, it gave her peace to know them just a little bit.

"Does it matter?" Emile asked.

She nodded, their eyes locking. "To me it does."

His eyes twinkled over his mask, and she knew he was smiling at her. "I forgot."

"What?"

"The connection you need and the peace you bring."

"It helps."

"Indeed," he whispered. "Thank you for reminding me."

"You're welcome, Doctor Moreau."

"Of course, Doctor MacDonald. Jasmine is Twin A and Ayesha is Twin B."

"Pretty names," she murmured.

Once again, looking into his eyes, she felt like she could see the old Emile again, staring at her across the operating room. It was like she'd been transported back in time, standing in front of the boy she'd been in love with all those years ago.

"Very pretty," Emile said faintly. Then he looked away, clearing his throat and breaking the spell. "Well, let's get ready."

Chloé approached the operating table and looked down at the babies. Her heart melted because they were so cute, so small and fragile.

She did love children. Sometimes she yearned to be a mother herself, but when would she have time? And there was a small part of her, deeply buried in the far corner of her heart, that was terrified at the prospect of having a child.

Of losing that child.

Her throat tightened as she thought about the parents of these twins, because she clearly remembered the pain and worry that seemed to be permanently etched on her own parents' faces every time Immi was in the hospital.

They'd come to visit Immitaq. She had rallied yesterday, battling her heart disease and they'd all been so hopeful.

But now Chloé knew. Even though she wasn't in the room with her parents, she could see them through the glass windows of the private room Immi's doctor had pulled them into.

Her heart sank.

The pain that had been gradually aging their mother, but had been partially held back, now erupted like a dam inside her had broken, flooding her face. Her father was no longer his jovial self. That was something she and Immi so loved about him—the way he made their days brighter. Now it was like every ounce of joy had been sucked out of his very being. His smile was replaced by pursed lips. His sparkling dark eyes devoid of that twinkle.

Chloé stared down at the book she'd brought for her sister, but she knew then Immi would never read it. In her heart, she knew that her twin, her other half, was gone.

She also knew she had to be the joy for her parents. She had lived when Immi hadn't. The least she could do was make sure she never added to their pain. So she swallowed her own.

Her parents needed her to be strong for them, even if it felt like she was crumbling; even if she barely knew how.

She was certain about one thing. She never wanted to feel the agony that her parents were going through.

"You ready?" Emile asked, interrupting her thoughts.

"Yes," Chloé said, smiling brightly from behind the mask and tearing her gaze away from the twins on the table. "Ready when you are, Doctor Moreau."

Emile was slightly surprised when Chloé just seemed to zone out while staring at the twins. He wasn't so shocked that she wanted to know the twins' names. He'd forgotten that sweet part of her. Maybe he'd buried it away deliberately, because there was no place for that kind of softness, not in his father's hospital. At one time, he'd liked to build up that personal connection with all of his patients, too, but once he'd stepped into his father's shadow, he'd had to lock away those bits and pieces of his personality.

Emile had known the twins' names, but sharing them with Chloé had felt special; it had changed the energy in the operating room to something hopeful.

Beautiful even.

Observing surgeons didn't usually ask for those kinds of personal details. They came to watch the procedures. And his father had *never* been one to form any kind of connection with a patient.

Not on that kind of level.

Everything in his father's life was business.

Cool.

Aloof.

Even his own private and familial relationships.

When his father had come to play the role of guest

surgeon at the hospital in Toronto where Emile had been doing his residency, he'd rounded with Emile and had not been pleased to see that his son had picked up that less than desirable habit.

"What're you doing?" his father demanded.

Emile was shocked. He'd been thrilled when his father took time out of his busy schedule as a visiting surgeon to do rounds with him, but now he'd pulled Emile into a meeting room. It seemed like his father was angry.

"Well?" his father asked again. "What're you doing, Emile?"

"Speaking to my patients?" Emile responded, confused.

"You're being too personal with them."

"Are you suggesting I be mean or cold with my bedside manner?"

His father's eyes narrowed. "No. You can be friendly, but don't make it personal. They're patients, not friends."

Emile was still confused. "Father, I guess I don't quite understand what you're getting at. I know they're not my friends."

"You're too chatty. Too friendly." His father frowned. "Do you want to one day be head of cardio at Hôpital de Ville-Marie?"

"Of course."

"You say that with hesitation."

"Father, I was pleased you came to see me. My attending is happy with my work..."

"That doesn't matter. What you need to do is

keep patients at a distance. You can't get too attached."

"I guess I don't understand, Father."

"You are their doctor. Their surgeon. Their life is in your hands. You're a professional, not their friend. They need to know you deserve their respect."

"I don't agree. They trust me."

Without even contemplating the fact that Emile could be right, his father shook his head. "You should've done your residency in Montreal. You're learning too many bad habits here. Hôpital de Ville-Marie is your legacy, a family legacy, and you will squander your chance to take your rightful place if you continue acting this way. Don't you want to make me proud?"

And that was the crux of it.

Emile shook the memory of his father out of his mind. He couldn't let it get to him. One of the reasons why he was one of the best cardiothoracic surgeons in Montreal was because he *did* have that personable connection with his patients. His patients all adored him. Frankly, it made him a better surgeon. It was one small piece that he kept from his time with Chloé, who was always so joyful and caring. Sometimes he liked to think that holding on to that empathy kept him connected to her, especially on days that he missed her.

His staff, on the other hand, might find him as cold and distant as his father. But to run his unit efficiently he had to be strict. What things would slip through the cracks if he really let down his guard?

He'd been out at lunch when those scans came in. A good chief of cardio would've been in radiology watching as the scans were being done. But instead…

Emile looked across the operating table at Chloé. Her dark eyes from behind that bright blue mask. Her dark lashes fanning her face. Her silken hair tied back under the scrub cap.

In that brief moment of admiring her, it felt like no time had passed. That he was still that young resident in Toronto, head over heels in love with her. The happiest times of his life.

Why had he thrown it all away?

But looking at Chloé, her accomplishments, her happiness, he just knew he'd made the right choice. This place and the person he'd become… Eventually, it would've ruined her and their love.

That, he could not bear.

Focus on the surgery, a little voice reminded him. *No time for doubts. Or for reminiscing over something you can't have.*

How quickly he was forgetting himself when he was around Chloé.

He had to shake all those thoughts out of his mind. His resident was reading off the information about the patients, about the operation they were going to perform, as Emile turned to the scrub nurse.

"Scalpel," he requested.

His preferred blade was handed to him and he set to work, because he was a surgeon first and foremost, living in the shadows of his family, and these little lives were in his hands.

Later, he could mull over the ghosts of his past, but nothing was going to change.

Chloé's home wasn't in Montreal and never would be. And that, as far as he was concerned, was for the best. She wanted a life he couldn't give her. Couldn't want for himself.

CHAPTER SIX

"COME CLOSER," Emile motioned to Chloé. She stepped forward. "I know I shouldn't ask a surgeon of your caliber to hold a clamp…"

"I would love to. Just like old times." Chloé stepped up and held a clamp where he instructed.

"You and Doctor MacDonald used to work together?" the resident on her left asked. Dr. LaCroix, Chloé remembered.

Emile shot him a "no small talk during surgery" look and Dr. LaCroix looked away.

"Don't be so grouchy, Doctor Moreau," Chloé answered brightly. "We did, in fact, Doctor LaCroix. We were residents together."

Emile groaned, but couldn't help smiling under his mask. "I forgot how you like to chat in theater, Doctor MacDonald."

"I do."

They shared a warm look across the table. He was half expecting her to start telling embarrassing stories about their days as residents, but she didn't.

He wouldn't mind reminiscing with her, just not around others. His residents didn't need to know about his personal life.

The operation went off without a hitch. He and Chloé worked seamlessly—which shouldn't shock him. When they were residents, they had always worked well together. But it was like no time had passed at all.

Sometimes, back then, they would butt heads, but for the most part they thought very similarly when it came to surgery and medicine. He'd forgotten what it was like to work with her and how much he enjoyed having her across from him in the operating room. He could get used to it.

She knew him before. She saw him as more than the head of the department here. He didn't have to earn her respect.

No. Don't think like that. I can't.

Emile had Dr. LaCroix close, and Chloé left the operating room while he worked on his operative report. Then he made his way to the post-anesthesia care unit to make notes on the twins' chart for the neonatal intensive care unit. He left detailed instructions for the nurses for the twins' post-op care. Jasmine and Ayesha were still under sedation and intubated so that they could fully recover. And he hoped that in a year they could be strong enough to be separated.

I wish Chloé would be here for that, too.

For a brief moment, he considered inviting her back.

He *tsked* under his breath and finished up his notes, annoyed that he was letting himself think like that again. Thinking of excuses or reasons to bring her back into his life.

Chloé was needed here to help with Céline and

they had agreed to be friends. Nothing more. It didn't have to be complicated.

The only risk was to his heart. Being around her made him forget himself, transported him right back to who he used to be, the man who had loved her so much.

Did you, though? If you loved her, you wouldn't have let her go.

In Emile's eyes, letting her go was the best thing he could've done, because at least now he wasn't holding her back—from her work, from everything she wanted.

"Father?" he asked, walking into his dad's study. Even at eighteen he felt like a child. His father was sitting in the dark staring at a photograph of Emile's mother.

"What is it?" his father asked. There was a clink of ice and Emile knew his father was drinking scotch, like he often did. There was a sense of sadness in the air.

"Why don't you call Mother?" Emile suggested.

"And why would I do that?"

"Because you miss her?"

And in one moment of clarity, his father's expression softened. "Oui. *I do, but we're too different. It was better to let her go. I loved her and set her free."*

"Why?" Emile asked.

His father shrugged and then looked away. "I love the hospital more."

And that was what Emile had done, too. It was for the best. For the both of them.

"Hey."

Emile turned around to find Chloé standing there. She had her coat on and her purse over her shoulder.

"You heading home?" he asked.

"Well, my home here in Montreal, yes." She grinned.

If only your home was here. A pang of longing hit him. But would having Chloé here really change anything in the grand scheme of things?

It wouldn't. Emile's stance on marriage and kids remained the same.

Why?

"I see," he stated, unsure of what to say or what to make of the emotions churning inside him.

"How are the twins?" she asked.

"Sedated, but their vitals are strong."

"Good. Thank you for allowing me to attend their repair today."

"Thank you for your help in the operating room." He set the chart back down at the nursing station for the NICU.

"I didn't do much," Chloé remarked.

"You did. It's easy to work with you. I'm glad that hasn't changed. Although, you had me worried."

"About what?"

"What were you going to say to Doctor LaCroix that might incriminate me?"

She chuckled, pink tingeing her cheeks, and tucked a strand of hair behind her ear. "Well, I'm going to head off. Céline is starting immunotherapy tomorrow and I want to get here early."

"What time does the immunotherapy start?"

"Six. Just after rounds."

"Well, then I think I'll be there as well. I would like to be there when immunotherapy starts. If I ever encounter heart cancer in a pediatric patient, I would like to know how to tackle it."

"You mean without having to call in the reserves?" she teased.

He smiled. "*Oui.* I suppose so."

They fell into step as they were leaving the NICU, not saying anything but walking in companionable silence, nothing like the awkwardness from before. Usually, when Emile was moving about the hospital, he was marching at top speed, always on a mission. He didn't really take strolls and definitely not with beautiful women. There was no time for that in his life.

Not that he would call walking through the hospital a stroll.

"What're your plans for dinner?" he found himself asking. He almost couldn't believe the words he was hearing, or that he'd been the one to say them. They just came spilling out of him before he had a chance to really think about it.

"I don't know," Chloé said. "I haven't had a chance to go shopping yet, so I was going to see what was around the residence hotel. Worse comes to worst I would have dinner in the hotel restaurant. Why?"

"Would you like to grab a bite to eat with me?"

What're you doing?

Emile didn't know, and judging by Chloé's stunned expression, she didn't, either. Apparently, he was having some kind of out-of-body experience.

But maybe this would be for the best; just bite the bullet and socialize. She had said friends were social. Dinner was social.

"Dinner?" she questioned.

"As friends," he reiterated. "I want to be your friend, Chloé. We were friends once before."

Chloé blushed again, then shook her head. "I want to be your friend, too, Emile. I enjoy spending time with you and I was glad when you reached out to me about this case."

"Good. I'm glad you want that. And of course I reached out to you. In this case, with respect to Céline, you are the best."

"I appreciate your frankness."

He cocked an eyebrow. "Really? Then you have certainly changed because in the past you didn't always appreciate that."

Chloé chuckled, and the awkward tension caused by the surprise dinner invite melted away. "Well, we're both older and wiser. Well, you're older."

He chuckled, unable to help it. "So, do you want to have dinner with me tonight? There's a great little restaurant down by the river."

"I would like that. It's a beautiful night and I would like to take in more of Montreal. Besides, I was going to take you up on the offer to go to Quebec City soon. Seeing how we're going to be friends, I thought it might be nice."

"*Bonne.* I'm glad for that. We can go this weekend if you're free?"

What are you doing? Dinner is one thing; a weekend getaway to another city is different.

"I am free. Unless something changes with Céline's case and I'm needed here, but that will most likely be the case the closer we get to surgery. Now might be the best time to go, when we're just starting out with her treatment. Would we have to stay overnight?"

"No. It's only three or so hours to Quebec City. But we can discuss all the details at dinner. How about I pick you up about seven at your hotel?"

Chloé nodded. "That sounds great. I'll see you then."

"Indeed."

Chloé walked away and Emile stood there for a few moments watching her, before the realization hit that he'd actually made a date with her.

Not a date. A friendly dinner between colleagues. He'd have to convince himself of that fact. Even if he'd never been out for dinner with anyone he'd worked with before.

He spent the next couple of hours trying to talk himself out of picking up Chloé. He half expected her to text him and try to get out of it herself, but she didn't. Finally, he just told himself to get over it. He truly did want to be her friend. And he'd enjoyed his lunch out with her.

A little too much. It had made him grapple with all those feelings he thought he'd locked away. But he wouldn't let that happen again tonight.

When they'd gotten back to the hospital after their lunch, he'd shut her out. Yet, try as he might, he couldn't keep away from her. It was clear he was lonely and the idea of having Chloé in his life in a platonic way was tempting.

It doesn't have to be more than that.

When he got back to his family's home, where he now lived, he realized the empty halls echoed a bit more than usual tonight. Most nights it didn't bother him, but right now it did.

Of course, it always was empty. Especially after his mother left. When it was just him and his father.

"You're too much like your father," his mother chided gently.

He briefly looked up from his work. "How so?"

"I've come to Montreal to visit you, but you're always working."

"I'm a surgeon."

"I know," his mother sighed sadly. "Why don't you take time off? Come to Beaupré for a break."

"Maybe."

Only he never had. He rarely saw his mother. He made sure she was taken care of, but time was not something he could give to her. There was an estrangement there. Why didn't he visit her? Why was he so afraid to leave the hospital work behind?

Because it's my life.

Now it was just him in this echoey old house, and

always would be. Because the work that meant he never saw his mother would never allow him to get married and have kids, either.

It cut him to the quick to think he was like his father; scared him. But then again, if he wasn't like him, Emile wouldn't be where he was now—wouldn't be the surgeon he was.

He was still mulling this all over in his head, when he realized with a jolt that he was pulling up to Chloé's hotel. It was like he had left the house and driven over in a trance.

But all those trepidations melted away the moment he saw Chloé, standing outside waiting for him. Like a beam of light at the end of a dark tunnel.

She took his breath away.

Just for a second. Just like the instant he'd seen her when she first entered the hospital, and time had stood still. Like she was frozen in a moment from their youth, when they had been so in love. When he'd been so happy.

Now he took another chance to watch her, taking it all in. She was wearing a flowy, flowery dress, sandals and a denim jacket. She looked chic and adorable. Perfect for a sultry summer Montreal night.

Emile smiled as she seemed to almost float toward the car. As much as he liked her in scrubs, she was gorgeous in a dress.

A dangerous thought. He had to be careful. He couldn't let memories or loneliness suck him back into thoughts of something more than friendship.

That wouldn't be fair to either of them.

This is exactly why I needed to keep my distance from her.

Too late for that now.

Chloé opened the door and slid in. The scent of her vanilla perfume wafted over Emile and he fought the urge to bury his face in her neck, her hair, to get lost in her arms like he had done so many times before.

"Thanks for picking me up, but I could've taken a taxi or something to the restaurant."

"It's not a problem," he replied, tearing his gaze away from her and gripping hard at the wheel. Friends out at dinner, nothing more. He had to keep replaying that mantra over and over in his head.

"Still, I could've met you there."

"It's kind of hard to do that when I didn't tell you where we're going," he said, smiling briefly.

"You didn't?" She glanced at her phone, scrolling. "Oh, you didn't. So where did I get that idea from?"

"Did you have a place in mind?" he asked, curious.

"Poire Romantique?"

"How do you know about *Poire Romantique*?"

"Well, I thought you told me." She shrugged. "So who knows where I got that from. Perhaps Céline's mom mentioned it when I stopped by to check on her before I left."

"That would make sense."

"Plus, I really like saying that name, *poire ro-*

mantique. Is it super exclusive or expensive? Is that why the premier recommended it?"

"Not really, but it's trendy. Hard to get into, but we can try, if you like," Emile stated.

"Well, where were you going to take me?" she asked.

"Does it matter now?"

"Sure it does." She smiled brightly at him. "Maybe I would like your place better?"

He chuckled. "And if you don't, I'll never hear the end of it."

"Ah, there's the old Emile," she said brightly.

"What do you mean?"

"You're so serious these days."

He bristled at her tone. "I run a department at the hospital. It's not a joke."

"I didn't mean to offend. I get it. I can't even begin to imagine."

"Thank you," he replied stiffly. Although, he understood her reasoning, her point.

It was hard to let loose. There was so much responsibility on his shoulders. A legacy baked into his DNA.

More like a burden.

"So where are we going?" Chloé asked, interrupting his morose thoughts.

"This little bistro down by the water that has an excellent duck confit and plays jazz."

"Oh, that sounds fun!" Chloé settled back against her seat. "Although, not sure how I feel about jazz. I'm more of a death metal gal."

"It's *light* jazz," he teased, correcting her. "I forgot you liked to head bang."

She stuck up her index and pinky, stuck out her tongue and shook her head, and he couldn't help but laugh.

"Give jazz a chance," he quipped.

"I swear I will."

It didn't take too long to get down to St. Paul Street and he parked the car in a garage. They walked a short couple of blocks to the bistro, *Choisir*. It was a beautiful summer's night. As the sun was setting, lights from the city reflected in the perfectly still waters of the St. Lawrence River. Light jazz floated out from the restaurant, creating an idyllic ambience. Emile couldn't remember the last time he'd really enjoyed himself like this, just walking down by the river on a summer night.

Maybe because I never have.

"This is cute," Chloé remarked as they came up to *Choisir*.

"I'm glad you think so," Emile remarked. He spoke quickly to the maître d' who stood outside and they were led inside the brick building that had originally been an old warehouse. It was warm and modern inside, and yet there was a retro speakeasy feel. It was one of Emile's favorite places, but he didn't often find time to come here.

It was the perfect place to take a date.

This is not a date.

How easy it was to slip back into old habits.

That's because you want to slip back.

* * *

Chloé's first impression of *Choisir* was how romantic it was. Nothing about this felt like a meal between friends. Of course, she wasn't exactly dressed for a work dinner, either, but since Emile had mentioned that he wanted to be friends, she'd chosen an outfit that she thought was completely casual, flirty and fun.

Nuka, not flirty. Not with Emile.

Chloé liked to flirt. It was fun. But even an innocent little flirt with Emile wasn't exactly safe. There was always a danger it could turn into something more. Chloé knew that firsthand, because that was what happened last time.

She slid into the booth that was tucked away in the corner. Emile slid in from the other side. The maître d' left them with menus, spoke some quick French that she couldn't pick up and then discreetly left.

The bar looked like a bootlegger's hideout, all exposed brick, dark wood and mirrors. And live jazz in a corner.

"Is this acceptable?" Emile asked, his blue eyes twinkling in the dim light. She'd always loved when they dazzled in her direction.

"We'll see. I mean, *Poire Romantique* was personally recommended to me by the premier of the province. If you can't trust a politician, who can you trust?"

A smile tweaked at the corner of his mouth, just

briefly before it vanished. "That's very facetious of you."

"I know." Chloé winked exaggeratedly, then instantly regretted it when Emile didn't laugh. "So, what's good here? I mean you said duck, but I'm not sure I want to eat Donald."

"What?" Emile asked, looking baffled.

"You know, the most famous duck I know."

Emile rolled his eyes. "Seriously?"

"I am being serious."

He sighed. "I forgot how weird you can be sometimes. Maybe I blocked it out."

"Okay, I'm sorry, weirdness aside. Duck confit sounds good, but I was hoping for some fish or seafood. Maybe something French."

"Duck confit is French," he said dryly.

"You're really pushing this duck on me, aren't you?"

"Fine. Foie gras?" he suggested.

"No. I can't in good conscience eat that. And besides, that's still duck, just its liver."

"You caught that, huh?"

"I'm not uncultured if that's what you think. I enjoy wild game and a good Alberta steak."

"Don't like jazz, prefers death metal. Rather have a burger." There was a hint of humor laced in there.

"Steak and hamburger are completely different."

"It's cow."

"Chopped and ground. Different."

"Salad Niçoise with the tuna is good," he mentioned, changing the subject.

"That sounds good." She closed her menu. "What're you getting?"

"Duck." There was a sparkle in his eyes and slight smile curled on his lips, hidden partially by the scruff of a beard he now wore.

Aloof, grumpy, whatever the others in the hospital called him, whatever he tried to be at work—deep down, Chloé could see that there were still pieces of the Emile she used to know; little glimpses that snuck out before he could quickly lock them away again.

The Emile she'd used to love.

Nuka, don't think like that, eh? Immi's voice warned in her head.

Her time here in Montreal was limited and she couldn't fancy herself falling for Emile again or give up on her goal and her commitment to Nunavut. She didn't want others in the north to face what her parents had, to have someone else lose their Immitaq.

Her whole career was centered around that goal and she couldn't walk away, just like she knew that Emile couldn't leave Montreal. It wasn't going to work for them.

It was annoying how easily she could be swayed by just a conversation with him; how much it made her want to allow those walls she'd built up to slip.

"*Bonjour*, I'm Henri and your waiter for this evening. Can I bring you some wine?" Henri asked, interrupting her train of thought.

"*Oui*, we'll have a bottle of your Crément de

Loire, Clos de Quaterons Chenin Blanc," Emile replied.

"Of course, monsieur." Henri scurried away.

"That sounded fancy," Chloé remarked. "White wine?"

"Champagne or something similar to champagne. It's *bulles*, or bubbles. I thought it might be nice to celebrate the successful procedure on the twins from earlier."

She nodded. "That's a good reason to celebrate."

Henri returned with their bottle on ice. There was a loud pop as he opened it and poured the sparkling wine into two glass flutes. "Are you ready to order?" he asked, placing the bottle back into the silver bucket.

"I think so," Chloé remarked.

"What would you like to order?" Henri asked.

"I'll have the Niçoise."

Henri nodded and turned to Emile. "Monsieur?"

"Duck confit." Emile handed him his menu.

"Very good. I'll return soon." Henri disappeared again.

Emile picked up his flute of *bulles* and held it up. "Cheers to our successes, both today and to come."

"Indeed." Chloé's hand shook slightly as their glasses clinked. She took a sip and then set the flute down on the table. "So, immunotherapy and chemo starts tomorrow for Céline."

"I saw the orders."

"I'm hoping that by the end of the month I can do the surgery." She fiddled with the fabric napkin on the table. "That being said, I have a patient from the north who I need to see. I was wondering if you'd had a chance to email the board about bringing my patients here?"

"I did. The premier also heard and said to do what it took to make it happen. They're quite willing to bring patients from Nunavut to Montreal."

"Good. I'll make the arrangements tomorrow, then." There was an awkward tension that fell between them. Suddenly, she didn't know what to say. "I was so shocked you asked me out to dinner."

"Trust me, I was shocked, too."

"Then, why?"

"Are you complaining?" he asked.

"No. Just…curious."

He nodded. "So am I."

She laughed nervously. "Well, we're off to a great start. You're just agreeing with me and we're not really talking about anything."

There was a brief half smile, one she always used to love, one that made her weak in the knees.

"Well, what do you think of my choice compared to the premier's?"

She looked around again. "This is a very cool spot. Trendy, you might say."

"It is indeed. It's one of my favorite places, but I don't come here often enough."

"Why not?"

Emile shrugged. "No time. I don't make time, I suppose. Work is my life."

"I hear that." And then even though she didn't

want to ask, she couldn't help herself. Maybe it was the bubbles talking. "So, no girlfriend, no dating?"

"No one." There was hesitation. "And how about you?"

"No. I'm very single. I guess work is my life, too. How sad is that?" Their eyes locked across the booth.

"I don't think it's sad," Emile said. "Look at what we do, the lives we save. I do love my work."

She smiled. "So do I, but don't you ever… I don't know, get lonely?"

She didn't know what she was hoping for with that line of questioning. Maybe *she* was the one who was lonely, though she never let it show. She was the master of a brave face, had been ever since they'd lost Immitaq, and her parents were so broken. Her happy face made everything okay.

And she'd gotten so used to it.

It was a bit nerve racking to sit here and let it slip, even a bit, to talk about loneliness with Emile.

"Yes, but my life does not allow me to devote time to a family. I won't do that to anyone." Emile looked away then, turning his head to look at the band playing in the corner. His lips pressed firmly together.

She'd definitely triggered something, but she didn't know what. She could recall him saying many times that he didn't want a family, didn't want kids, when they were residents. He'd told her he could never commit to that, even though he knew it was something she wanted.

Yet, back then he'd wanted her.

Until he hadn't.

The pain she felt at the memory of the breakup was fresh and startling, enough to steal her breath.

She had to be more careful here tonight.

For the rest of the dinner she steered the conversation toward work. There were no more personal discussions and Chloé was relieved. It was easier to block out all those old feelings about Emile when she could keep him at a professional distance.

When the food came, she kind of regretted not getting the duck because it looked amazing, but she enjoyed her salad nonetheless.

When dinner was over, they split the bill, like friends would do. Chloé reflected that she would eventually have to find a place to pick up groceries; her hotel suite had a little kitchen and she really couldn't eat out every night for the next month. Even though she wouldn't mind coming back to *Choisir*.

"So that wasn't too bad, was it?" Emile asked as they strolled at a leisurely pace back to where his car was parked.

"No. It was wonderful."

"Even with jazz?" A smile curled on his lips.

She laughed softly. "Yes, even with jazz."

As they walked along the city streets, she could hear the sound of a ship in the distance. For a brief moment, it reminded her of home, of the remote village along Hudson's Bay they'd lived in before they'd moved to Iqaluit. The big cargo ships would come in near their house, laden with supplies that couldn't be flown in, and it had been so exciting to watch them carve through the icy waters.

"You're smiling. What're you thinking about?" Emile asked.

"Home."

"Oh?"

She nodded and pointed over her shoulder toward the water. "The ships on the river. It reminded me of the ones that came up to the little inlet where I lived when I was a kid. Immi and I…" She trailed off, thinking of her sister. "We'd all be excited."

Emile didn't question her about Immi, and she was relieved. She never told him about her sister, and she didn't want to talk about her tonight.

"Would you like to take a walk down by the river?" he asked.

No.

A moonlit walk with Emile didn't seem very smart. But instead of being smart, she said, "Sure."

Emile placed his hand on the small of her back, guiding her down a side street toward the promenade that overlooked the water. His touch sent a shiver of anticipation coursing through her, her body coming alive at such a simple yet intimate movement. The river was still, but they could see the moving lights of one of those big ships coming in.

Chloé leaned over the railing, drinking in the fresh air. The St. Lawrence was where fresh water from the Great Lakes met with the ocean, so there was a hint of brine on the air.

"I wonder where they're going," she said out loud.

"Nunavut," Emile remarked.

She glanced up at him. "Really?"

He nodded. "Did you not know that those ships from your childhood came from here?"

"I was eight. I wasn't really tracking it."

He smiled. "I suppose not when you're that young."

"We were more concerned about who in town would be getting a new truck or toys or something."

"Hmm, growing up here I never really thought of waiting for a car to come in on a ship."

"I guess not. You have access to the Trans-Canada Highway. Nunavut does not."

Emile leaned over next to her. They were so close, their arms almost brushing as they stared out over the water.

Chloé felt exposed talking about her past like this, when he was so silent. "Tell me about your childhood," she said.

"Why?" he asked, cocking an eyebrow.

"You never really told me much. All we did was study and make out." Heat flushed in her cheeks. That last part was just blurted out, without her conscious permission.

Oh, Nuka.

Emile grinned. "Those weren't terrible days."

She groaned, straightening up. "I'm so sorry."

"For what?"

She shot him a look. "Seriously."

Emile laughed then, out loud. "It's okay, Chloé."

"Is it?"

He stood in front of her, his hands resting on her forearms. He stared deep into her eyes and suddenly she wasn't embarrassed anymore. Instead, her body reacted to his touch, to his smile, to everything.

"Those were some of my favorite days," he said softly.

"Mine, too," she whispered, her heart racing.

Emile reached out and gently ran his knuckles over her cheek. She closed her eyes, reveling in his touch. The warmth. The heat. Her lips parted, and then she felt his mouth against hers. Just a light brush first, and then something deeper as his arms wrapped around her. She crushed him to her body, her fingers trailing in the hair at the nape of his neck. Her body thrumming happily as it remembered his kisses, even after all this time.

Emile froze in her arms. Then he stepped back. "I'm sorry."

"For what?" she asked. Though she didn't know why. She knew she shouldn't be kissing him, either, but her body longed for more and she wanted to be back in his arms, even if it was wrong.

"That shouldn't have happened," he said quickly. He wasn't looking at her. His body rigid like he'd locked down every ounce of softness.

"Well, it did."

He shook his head. "We're working together. This can't happen."

It was like he was angry with her, which hurt for a moment, alongside the sting of rejection. But he was right. This couldn't happen again, and Chloé *knew* that. Nothing had really changed. He was here; she was needed up north. He didn't want kids; she did.

Even if it hadn't happened for her yet.

She pushed that thought away. She still had a lot of work to do before she settled down. She was doing something with her life and not squandering it.

And if she let a kiss that could go nowhere happen again or, worse, if she allowed herself to hope for anything more, she would be wasting her time. Time best spent on her work.

"You're right," she said, finding her voice. "It won't."

Emile nodded, but still wouldn't look her in the eye. "I better take you back to the hotel."

"I think that's wise."

They walked quickly back to his car. In silence.

Chloé was so mad at herself for falling so fast into that trap. It hurt to drag herself back out, just like she'd known it would, but she had to put on a brave face, press on. She was stronger than heartache.

What she had to do was pretend like this night had never happened. For Céline's sake and for her own.

Emile dropped her at the hotel and she quickly went back to her suite.

As much as she tried to sleep and put that amazing yet regret-tinged kiss out of her mind, she just couldn't. She spent the night tossing and turning again, replaying it over and over, wrestling with all the emotions that Emile could easily stir up in her.

When she got up the next morning, she had made the resolution that she wasn't going to go to Quebec City with him this weekend. He kept saying that he wanted to be friends and she'd thought she wanted that, too, but she was finding it too hard. Whenever work was off the table, other things began to creep in, like that perfect, terrible kiss.

There was no way she was going to put her heart on the line like that again. Even though she'd absolutely *loved* it. She couldn't be foolish or selfish.

When she got to her office, she sat down with a sigh. At least, burying herself in work would help her to ignore all these racing thoughts. Medicine grounded her completely. All she had to do today was focus on that and get her head on straight.

"Chloé, I hope I'm not disturbing you?"

Chloé groaned inwardly as the very man she was trying to avoid this morning was standing in her doorway. She hadn't even heard him knock. "Ah, Emile. I just got in and was about to go over Céline's chart from the rounds this morning."

She was hoping he'd take the hint and leave her to work, because right now she didn't really want to see him. What she needed was space.

"I'll just be a moment. It's about this weekend…"

"You don't have to say any more," she responded quickly. "I have to run back to Ottawa for some things I forgot. Hopefully, we can go to Quebec City another time."

She was giving him an easy out. It was for the

best to put some distance between them. It was the only way to keep things professional in the long run.

Emile looked relieved. "Oh good. I was coming to give you my regrets about it. I have some work I need to do."

"No regrets or apologies needed. We both have busy schedules."

An awkward tension fell between them. Chloé hated it. Emile was barely looking at her, yet he still lingered, like he wanted to say more, but didn't speak.

"So," she said, hoping her voice didn't break. "Work."

"Indeed. Well, I'll leave you to it."

Just as Emile turned, she got a buzz on her phone. It was about Céline, who was starting her chemotherapy. Emile glanced at his own phone, obviously getting the notification, too.

They exchanged a worried look.

There was no time for personal weirdness. All that could wait. Chloé jumped up, grabbing her white lab coat and stethoscope and following after Emile quickly. They didn't say anything as they ran through the halls, heading to the pediatric oncology department where Céline would be receiving her treatment.

Agathe, Céline's mother, was pacing outside the room. A code blue had been called and residents were working on Céline.

Chloé entered the room, clinging on to her calm,

drowning out the excitement around her so she could focus.

“Give me an update,” she shouted over the throng.

“Cardiac tamponade,” a resident stated. “Patient’s heart rate went up after her first infusion of chemotherapy this morning. Patient complained of shortness of breath. We did an ultrasound of her chest and saw the fluid.”

Chloé studied the images quickly and then leaned over Céline, who was on the stretcher, unconscious. It was cardiac tamponade during the night that had killed Immitaq. There had been no one there to help relieve the pressure of fluid in the pericardial sac, and her heart couldn’t pump under the pressure of the fluid buildup.

She listened to Céline’s breathing and noticed the bulging neck veins. The heart was beating fast still and she would have to work quickly to get the fluid out from around it.

“What do we do?” Chloé asked Dr. LaCroix, the resident who had done the ultrasound.

“Pericardiocentesis,” Dr. LaCroix stated.

“You’re correct. I need an operating room booked stat. Start Céline on a course of antibiotics. Doctor LaCroix, you’re the one who caught the tamponade—I want you in the room with me while I perform it.”

“Yes, Doctor MacDonald,” Dr. LaCroix answered.

“Have Céline down to the OR in twenty minutes. This needs to happen now.” Chloé stood up and headed out of Céline's room where Emile was speaking to Agathe.

"Well?" Agathe asked, her face pale. "What happened? I thought the chemotherapy was supposed to help her."

"It will," Chloé responded calmly. "Due to the severity of her cancer, the chemotherapy caused fluid to build up in the pericardium, the lining around her heart. That fluid buildup was making it hard for her heart to pump blood adequately. With your permission I would like to take Céline into the operating room and perform a pericardiocentesis to drain the fluid from around her heart so we can continue treatment."

Agathe nodded, her eyes filled with unshed tears. "Do what you have to do."

"I'll have the consent forms drawn up," Emile stated firmly, disappearing.

Agathe ran her hands over her face. "This shouldn't be happening."

Chloé reached out and squeezed Agathe's hand. "No. It shouldn't be. Not to someone so young, but unfortunately it's common in patients like Céline. At least we caught it—sometimes people aren't that lucky. Or they don't have access to the health care or hospitals. Remote communities up north."

She hadn't meant to say that, but all she saw in this moment was Immitaq.

"Please," Agathe whispered. "Help her."

"Try not to worry about Céline. I will take good

care of her and I will let you know when the procedure is done."

Agathe nodded again.

Chloé made her way to the operating room floor. Céline was already in the operating room and prepped, ready to go. Chloé would review the chemotherapy dosing with pediatric oncology after she did the procedure and decide whether or not she would have to adjust Céline's dose. Cardiac tamponade didn't just happen spontaneously; it had probably been building up since her last scan. She was just glad to be here to catch it and treat it.

As she took a deep breath, she closed her eyes and saw Immi's smiling face. A face so like her own. One she missed. Her other half.

She'd do this for Immi.

Emile got the consent forms for Chloé to do the procedure on Céline.

He'd only gone to her office this morning to call off the Quebec City trip, and had been pleased when she was the one to cancel first. After dinner last night and that kiss, it had become apparent to him quite quickly that being social with her outside of work was just going to be too difficult.

Every moment he spent with her made it far too easy to slip into old habits. So easy to forget to keep her at arm's length. Mostly because he didn't want to.

That kiss had been everything. She'd tasted just as sweet as he remembered. But it had also been a mistake. It had been so hard to end it, but he'd had to step away.

It was for the best.

After he dropped her off at her hotel he'd gone back to his home and just thought about her all night. Once again, not getting any sleep. Ever since he called her to come in and deal with this case, he hadn't been sleeping well.

Just talk to her.

What was he going to say to her? *I don't want to hang out with you outside of work because I can't stop thinking about you? I've never stopped thinking about you?*

He scrubbed in and headed into the operating room to check on how the pericardiocentesis was going. It was hard seeing young children as heart patients, but to see Céline as a heart patient with cancer, especially such an aggressive one, was even more difficult.

The fluoroscopy was up and running and Chloé had just gotten the drain inserted into the pericardium.

"How is it going?" Emile asked.

"Good. I'm glad Doctor LaCroix here was able to spot the cardiac tamponade when he was checking over her vitals after her round of chemo."

Dr. LaCroix briefly looked up at her. "Thank you, Doctor MacDonald."

Emile glanced at him. "Well, I'm glad to hear that."

Dr. LaCroix nodded and continued his work.

Chloé looked askance over him. "I think it's a job well done for your residents."

"*Oui*," Emile agreed, but he didn't say anything further. His father had taught him that you train the best surgeons in this program by being cool and distant, not so heavy on the praise. When Emile had come here after his residency in Toronto, he'd had to shake a lot of bad habits.

Even though his father was gone, the surgeons his father had trained still treated Emile the same cold way his father had treated them, the way his father would treat him. Emile knew that he had a reputation, a family legacy to live up to.

It was why he'd worked so hard to become the youngest head of cardiothoracic surgery in this hospital. He was always striving to make his father proud. But it was hard to make someone who was no longer alive proud.

"Tough crowd," Chloé muttered under her breath.

Dr. LaCroix chuckled, but only for a moment before he caught Emile's eye again and went back to his work.

"Are you going to adjust Céline's medications?" Emile asked, ignoring the slight barb from her.

"I will get the fluid tested and make sure there was no infection that caused the fluid to build up around her heart, but yes, most likely. I want to avoid this happening again. I need her heart as strong as I can get it to do the surgery. Cardiac tamponade is an unwanted complication."

"Indeed." Emile watched the fluoroscopy images

as the fluid was drained slowly away. There wasn't much he could do in this moment. "How are her vitals?"

"Improving," Chloé offered. There was a hint of hope, but also a bit of sadness in her voice as she said it. "Kids are resilient."

"They are."

"No matter how hard my sister's treatment was…" She trailed off and he could see the bloom of pink flush in her cheeks. She cleared her throat. "Anyway, yes, kids are resilient."

The comment caught him off guard. A sister? He could tell by Chloé's reaction that she hadn't meant to let that slip out.

"I didn't know about your sister," he said tentatively. "Does she have heart troubles?"

"Had," Chloé replied stiffly. "Had a sister."

Then before Emile could ask anything else, she moved closer to Céline and continued her work on the delicate procedure. Just from her body language, he knew that the conversation was closed.

He was shocked. All through their residency and their time together, she'd never once mentioned her sister.

Had a sister. There was pain in those words. One he'd never heard in her voice before.

It was obviously a sore spot. But still, why had she hidden that information? Why hadn't she talked about it with him before?

Was it really so surprising? There were things about his personal life Emile had never told her.

Things he kept hidden and didn't want to share. When they'd gotten together in the first place, both of them had known that they were going in different directions, and so why open up?

What they'd had together had been fun and easy. It was never supposed to be more. Even though, at points he'd wished it could have been. Still wished it, sometimes.

"Well," he said, clearing his throat. "I would like to be kept informed on Céline's status. Let me know when the procedure is done so I can inform her parents."

"I'll keep you updated," Chloé replied brightly. "Another thirty minutes and the fluid should all be drained and we'll have her in recovery."

Whatever sadness that had passed over her when she talked about her sister was now gone. There was no need to dive deeper or get to know her any further. She clearly didn't welcome it, and there was no point.

Emile left the operating room, scrubbed out. He was working on his notes, waiting, when Chloé finally came out and found him.

"Well?" he asked.

"Céline is on her way to the PACU. I've sent the fluid off for testing. Shall we go tell Agathe and Tomas the good news?"

"Oui."

They found Céline's parents in the waiting room. They both stood when Emile and Chloé entered.

"She's in recovery," Chloé announced. "She's

strong and I've sent the fluid off for testing. Once we have those answers we'll adjust the treatment."

Agathe and Tomas hugged each other.

"When can we see her?" Tomas asked.

"Soon," Emile responded.

Agathe relaxed and straightened her sweater. The worried mother, transitioning back to put-together politician. "Doctor MacDonald, thank you," she said. "You're clearly talented."

"Flattery is not needed," Chloé stated. "It's nice, but not required."

"Oh, when I see talent I take hold of an opportunity," Agathe explained. "Earlier you mentioned something about northern communities."

Chloé's eyes widened. "I did."

"We have a remote northern Quebec community that is struggling right now. We can't keep staff. We fly surgeons up there when we can. There are several heart patients waiting. When I was sitting here, I was thinking about that. I would like you both to go up there to help."

"I would be happy to give up a few days to visit your patients up north," Chloé responded enthusiastically.

Agathe smiled. "You would?"

Chloé nodded. "I'm from a remote community, although my family lives in Iqaluit now. It can be hard to keep staff and sometimes the infrastructure doesn't support it. If I can help out while I'm here, then I would love to."

"How about you, Doctor Moreau?" Agathe asked. "Can the hospital spare you for a couple of days?"

Emile totally understood why Chloé would agree to that, and part of him yearned to do the same. But he wasn't sure how he felt about being in a remote community with just her. Riding in a bush plane with just her.

At least it's only for a day, to see some patients and assess them. That's it.

"Of course," he said, but not with the same enthusiasm as Chloé.

Agathe nodded. "I'll arrange it and let the community know. Having two cardiothoracic surgeons of both your calibers up there attending to the community would be a huge boon. And as you're familiar with northern communities, I would love to get a report on what the government of Quebec could do to further strengthen our communities up there."

Chloé gave Emile a strange look, but she was still smiling. "Well, I'm going to go check on Céline. I will send a nurse out to get you both when it's okay to see her."

"Yes. I better go on my rounds." Emile went in the opposite direction. He was still in shock that he'd agreed to go up north with Chloé.

He shouldn't have done it. He had too many responsibilities here. But it was something he'd always wanted to do.

It would only be for a day or two. Max. I can handle that.

As he was thinking about it, a charge nurse in the

PACU came rushing up to him. "Doctor Moreau, your assistant Donna has just phoned about an urgent call."

"An urgent call?"

The nurse nodded. "Your mother is in the hospital."

"My mother?" he asked, confused.

Why was his mother in Montreal? He hadn't seen her in five years. She didn't like coming to the city and he didn't go visit her.

"Donna is on line three."

"*Merci.*" Emile quickly ran over to the nursing station desk and picked up the phone. "Donna?"

"Doctor Moreau, your mother has been admitted to the cardio ward and she's requesting to see you. She's on floor four in room 104B."

"I will be there straightaway." Emile hung up the phone. Of all the things he'd thought he would have to face today, his mother being admitted to the hospital was not on his bingo card.

He sped quickly to the private room where his mother had been admitted. He didn't even knock, just barged into her room, startling the nurse who was taking her vitals.

"Emile," his mother said, surprised. "You scared us."

Not a word about "I haven't seen you in a long time" or any explanation about why she was in Montreal. All she did was chastise him about startling her.

"What're you doing here, Maman?"

His mother looked so small in the hospital bed. Her long white hair braided over her shoulder and her blue eyes, which usually sparkled, were dull. There were dark circles under her eyes. She gave off the appearance of being frail, which was never a good sign.

"Well, that's a pleasant way to say hello. I haven't seen you in five years and this I how you greet your *mère*? Just barging into her hospital room and asking her what she's doing here?"

Emile sighed and glanced at the nurse.

"I'll be back later," the nurse said, discreetly exiting.

Emile crossed his arms and watched her leave. "Maman—"

"You scared off that poor nurse," his mother chastised.

"Maman," Emile stated firmly. "I mean, what're you doing in Montreal?"

"I was in town for an art exposition. Some of my work is being featured at a gallery and I collapsed. My heart was racing and they couldn't bring it down, so I was brought here where a cardiologist had me admitted. Then I had you paged, as you're a heart doctor."

Emile sighed and pulled up her chart. "I can't be your heart doctor, though. Besides, I'm a surgeon. I don't even know if you need a surgeon."

"Oh, I do," his mother said offhandedly. "Something about a block in an artery? I don't know. I lived with your father for many years and I could never keep up with the medical terminology. Just like he had no interest in my art."

He softened as he flipped through her chart. He could see the note from her physician in Beaupré that she did indeed need an angioplasty and that her doctor had recommended it a year ago. Her arteries were blocked: the procedure would allow the surgeon to widen the arteries and improve blood flow, not only to her heart but also to other parts of her body. He wondered if she was having any kind of numbness or tingling.

"Maman, Doctor Boulanger said you needed an angioplasty a year ago, but you didn't have it done? Why didn't you tell me?"

His mother shrugged. "I feel fine. Besides, you're always working. I didn't want to burden you."

Instantly, he felt crushing guilt. "Maman…"

"Emile, I'm fine. I'm not angry at all. You don't have to fuss."

Emile took a deep breath. "You're clearly not well. I'm booking you in for an angioplasty."

"I thought you couldn't do my surgery?"

"I can't, but I can have another surgeon here at the hospital perform it. It's a minimally invasive procedure. You could've had it done in Beaupré or in Quebec City. When Doctor Boulanger told you to."

"Well, I'm here now." His mother smiled. "It is good to see you. Still married to your work, I see?"

Emile grunted, but then smiled down at her. "I'm sorry I haven't been out to visit."

"You're like your father that way."

"So you tell me," he groused. "Well, I'm going to find a surgeon to help you. You're admitted, officially."

"So much for the gallery," she sighed sadly.

Emile felt a pang of sympathy for her. He bent over and kissed her quickly on the head. "I'll come by and visit you later."

"I would like that."

Emile stepped out of the room, texted Chloé to call him and scrubbed his hands over his face, leaning against the wall for a brief moment to catch his breath. Right now he couldn't keep his emotions under control. He felt like he was spinning like a whirling dervish. His phone buzzed and he answered it.

"Hey, Céline is waking up," Chloé said, bubbly. "I'm very happy with her recovery."

"That's good," he said.

"So you wanted me to call?"

"*Oui.*" He cleared his throat, hoping his voice didn't break, because in that moment he just couldn't control his exhaustion.

"What's wrong?" Chloé asked softly on the other end.

There was a part of him that didn't want to tell her, but this was his mother, and Chloé was a good surgeon. If he couldn't do the angioplasty, he could have one of the best cardiothoracic surgeons in Ontario and Nunavut do the procedure.

He trusted her.

What he wanted to tell her was that he needed

her. He needed a good surgeon and he needed a friend. But he locked that all inside, didn't let it out.

"Would you come up to floor four, the cardiac ward? I have a case I need to discuss with you."

"Sure. I'll be there soon."

Emile ended the call and tried to collect himself.

Not just a good surgeon, not just a friend. He needed *Chloé* in this moment. As much as he didn't want to, he did need her. Now more than ever.

CHAPTER SEVEN

CHLOÉ WAS SURPRISED by Emile's call. Especially after she had just seen him. Her first thought was to wonder why he needed an update so soon. Then she thought maybe he wanted a chat about going up north, since Agathe had kind of surprised them both with the offer. Chloé had been shocked that he'd actually said yes.

Then she'd heard his voice over the phone. He'd sounded completely distraught, completely unlike anything she'd heard from him before, even from their residency days. She couldn't help but wonder what was up.

She hoped it wasn't about her admission in the operating room. He'd seemed so concerned about that.

She really didn't want to talk about her late sister with him. She was still kicking herself letting that bit of information slip, because she didn't tell anyone about Immitaq. That was her burden alone to bear. Anytime she'd tried to bring up her sister as a child, it had always brought so much pain to her parents that she'd just learned not to talk about it. There was no need to upset them.

The only person she talked to about Immi was herself. There was no reason to hide behind a mask of happiness when she was alone.

Yet, seeing Céline there, going through the exact same thing that had killed her sister, it had been so hard not to think about Immi. She'd slipped up and couldn't be more annoyed with herself.

If Emile wanted to talk about Immitaq, she would just have to put a stop to it. It was too personal. She'd never shared it with him back when they were dating, and she wasn't going to open up about it now. It was too intimate.

The last thing she needed to do was have him think differently about her. He seemed to view emotions as a weakness, because he was so good at locking them up tight, and she didn't want to appear vulnerable in front of him or have him think that somehow she wasn't strong enough.

But why had he sounded so lost on the phone? She wanted to reach out and comfort him, like she did when her own parents were in pain.

Slippery slope, Nuka. Slippery slope.

When she found him at the nursing station, she actually took a step back. He was slouched in his chair, his head in his hand, aimlessly staring at a chart. He seemed distraught. Not his usual collected self. It threw her off. She'd never seen him like this.

He looked up and just appeared to be exhausted. "Oh good. You're here."

"Of course I am. What's up?"

He handed her a chart, his mouth set in a firm line. "Take a look at this."

Chloé cocked an eyebrow but opened the chart

on the tablet he handed her. She quickly scanned the assessment with imaging.

"What do you think?" he asked, his voice quiet.

"I agree with this diagnosis. An angioplasty should be done right away."

"And the patient waited a year!" Emile snapped, in a strange burst of emotion.

Chloé looked again. "Indeed, that was kind of ballsy of her, given her age of seventy-eight."

"It was foolish," he seethed, running his hand through his hair. He was really worked up. Angry almost, which also seemed not like him.

"Marguerite Angenoux. Do you know her? And by that I mean personally?"

"I do. She's my mother."

Now it was Chloé's turn to be stunned at brand-new information. "Your mother?"

Logically, she knew Emile had a mother; it was just that he never mentioned her. Or if he did, it was rare. She had a vague recollection that she'd come up in conversation the other night, but from the way Emile had spoken of her, Chloé had thought she had passed.

"She divorced my father when I was young," Emile said, "and she moved out to Beaupré. My father had custody of me. My mother is a…a free spirit."

"Oh really?" She tried to say it in a way that wasn't facetious, but she couldn't help but think of all those memes of a surprised feline because she felt just as shocked as that ridiculous cat. She had a hard time picturing Emile being raised by a flower child.

Emile sent her a quelling glance. “Don’t sound so surprised.”

“You just never talked about your mother much.” Chloé scrolled through the chart again. “So, what would you like me to do about it?”

“I would like you to do the angioplasty.”

“Me? Any surgeon here could do that surgery. A resident…” She trailed off as Emile crossed his arms and glared at her in frustration. “Right, not a good idea. Sure, if you want me to do the angioplasty, then I can do that for you. Tomorrow. I see the cardiologist who admitted her has started all the correct pre-procedure medications and she’s on blood thinners, so yeah, I can do the angioplasty early tomorrow, if that’s okay with her.”

“It’s okay with me,” Emile stated quickly.

Chloé grinned at him. “Ah, but is your mother of sound mind?”

“Well, that’s debatable, as she waited so long to get the angioplasty,” he groused.

“Oh my, we’re grumpy,” she teased. “I need to call you Oscar.”

“Chloé,” he said in exasperation.

“I’m sorry.”

“So you’ll do it?”

“I have to get her consent,” Chloé stated again. “So, I really do think I need to meet her.”

“You want to meet my mother?”

She smiled brightly. “Well, if I’m going to perform her angioplasty then yes, I probably should meet her. Ah, she's in room 104B. Perfect."

As she headed in the direction of the room, Emile came running up beside her and grabbed her elbow, pulling her around. "I never told her about us."

"Us?" Chloé teased, which just made Emile frown.

"Chloé," he warned.

"Relax, we're friends, right? Colleagues. I'm just that particular colleague you've seen naked."

She probably shouldn't have said that, but she always did enjoy teasing him. It was a coping mechanism she used to lighten the mood. And the mood definitely needed it right now.

"Chloé," he sighed.

"Don't worry. I'm a surgeon and I'll be professional. I'll take care of your mother." Chloé knocked on the door and opened it when she heard a faint voice telling her to come in. Emile followed on her heels.

Emile's mother had his blue eyes and the same smile. She was smiling now, but looked so exhausted resting against the pillows, slightly elevated in the hospital bed. Instantly, Chloé could see there was some swelling in her hands, possibly from arthritis, possibly from the blockage.

"Hi, Madame Angenoux. I'm Doctor Chloé MacDonald. I'm a surgeon and a colleague of your son's."

"Oh, it's a pleasure to meet you. Please call me

Marguerite." She held out her hand and Chloé took it, gently shaking it, feeling the swelling there.

"And you can call me Chloé. I like a bit of informality with my patients." She could practically hear Emile's teeth grind.

Marguerite smiled brightly and then glanced over at Emile. "I like this surgeon."

"Mother, Doctor MacDonald would like to perform your angioplasty tomorrow morning," Emile said tightly.

Marguerite turned her attention back to Chloé. "How long will I be in the hospital for?"

"A couple of days, and then your son can take you home. But then I would like to see you in a week, just to check up on you postoperatively." Chloé stood up. "Can I listen to your chest?"

"Of course." Marguerite tried to sit up but struggled.

Chloé helped her and then listened. Her breath was labored, but her chest sounded clear, just not her heart. "Thank you, Marguerite."

"So this checkup. If I go home to Beaupré, it's quite the trip to come back in a week. I don't drive and I think the train might be too difficult if I'm recovering from surgery."

"You're right," Chloé agreed. "Well, since I'm a visitor here for a short time and you're the mother of a friend, I think I can make the trip out to see you myself."

"A house call?" Emile asked, stunned.

Chloé shrugged. "Sure. Why not? I do them all

the time in Nunavut. Sometimes, it's just easier to go to the patient rather than dragging the patient to the hospital."

Marguerite beamed brightly. "Oh, I like her. And Nunavut? How exciting. I used to study the artwork of Kenojuak Ashevak when I was in university. I met them once when they came to Ottawa."

"How exciting! I do love Kenojuak's works," Chloé stated.

"I think it's quite all right if you perform the surgery. You're much more personable than my late husband and my son, who hasn't visited me in five years." Marguerite looked at her son pointedly.

Emile groaned and rolled his eyes.

Chloé laughed quietly. "Is that true, Emile?"

"I'm a busy surgeon and head of a department at a busy hospital."

"Yes. We know," Chloé stated.

"I'm only teasing, Emile," Marguerite said, winking at Chloé.

"I think your son might've reminded you that you should've had this taken care of a year ago," Chloé said gently.

Marguerite sighed. "I know, but I was busy and it just seemed like a nuisance."

"Now you sound like your son," Chloé said lightly, making Marguerite smile.

"Maman, your health is not a nuisance," he said firmly, with a hint of tenderness.

Chloé nodded. "I have to agree with your son on this."

"My apologies then for being such a trouble." Marguerite sighed, leaning back.

"Well, it'll be taken care of now," Chloé said softly.

"Thank you both." Marguerite nodded.

"I'll see you tomorrow," Chloé said.

"Get some rest, Maman." Emile opened the door and they left Marguerite's room. As he shut the door, Chloé stifled a grin.

"Well, for being your mother, she's not what I expected," she said.

"And what did you expect?" he asked with an exasperated tone.

"I don't know, someone not so…friendly and agreeable. Then again, you did say she was a free spirit. Still, I see some similarities."

"How so?"

"She's stubborn. So are you. She waited a year and is only here because she collapsed."

"I see your point."

"She's lovely, though, Emile."

"She's only nice to you because it's you and not me." He let out a sigh. "She's very well liked. It was my father who was a bit cold and aloof. I honestly question why those two got together in the first place."

"Chemistry?" she suggested.

Emile made a face. "I don't want to think about my parents having any sort of chemistry."

She laughed. "I'm sorry. Like I say, she's lovely. I don't mind doing the angiogram."

"I appreciate it. Truly, I do."

They both started to walk away. Chloé could tell that he was bothered by something, yet not telling her what it was.

The weirdness about the kiss from last night, meanwhile, seemed to be a forgotten point on his side, and that was fine by her. It was just best to pretend it didn't happen. Except, it was a hard thing for her to forget, because she kept seeing it in her mind.

She could taste it on her lips. Her blood heated.

Nuka, stop!

"Hey, family is complicated," she said, breaking the silence. "And the angioplasty will go smoothly. From what I can tell by just glancing at your mother's chart, besides the blockage, she's in fairly good health. A couple of days to recover here and then you can take her home. I don't recommend sending her home on the train."

"Agreed. I will take her home."

"Do you want me to help?" She couldn't believe the words were coming from her mouth, but now they were out there. Even though they had both *just* agreed to cancel their friendly trip to Quebec City, here she was now offering to help take his mother home, which was on the other side of Quebec City.

Nuka, this is not keeping your distance.

Emile raised his eyebrow in surprise. "You would help me do that?"

She shrugged. "It's an excuse to see more of the province."

"What about the stuff you needed to attend to in Ottawa this weekend?"

She worried her bottom lip and grinned. "It was an excuse?"

Emile chuckled. "So was mine… I thought it would be better."

"This is foolish, though. We can be friends. I want to be your friend, Emile. You asked me to help out with your mother and that's what friends are for. Let's forget last night happened." Not that looking at him now, so worried about his mother, was helping with that resolution. It was a little glimpse of that tender side of Emile. The one she'd loved once.

His expression softened for a moment again. "You're right. I would appreciate the company on the drive to Beaupré."

"Great. Then it's settled. I'll add your mother to the operating room schedule for tomorrow morning and then this Saturday we'll take her back home and get her comfortable."

"That sounds good."

"I'm going to head down to oncology and talk to them about Céline's chemotherapy and make sure pathology is rushing the test of that fluid we took from her pericardium. I'll talk to you later." Chloé quickly scurried away.

She was pleased that he'd asked for her help with his mother and that they were both able to admit that they'd been giving each other excuses on why they were backing out of the weekend day trip to Quebec City. It was apparent they were both on the same page about their feelings toward one another and the need to just keep everything platonic.

The problem now was: Why did that thought just sting a little bit?

Thankfully, Chloé was able to focus on her work the rest of the day. She was able to adjust and order another round of chemotherapy for Céline, then get Emile's mother on the operating room schedule for six in the morning. For the rest of the day she focused on her reports and didn't see Emile again.

When she got back to her hotel that night she ordered in dinner and finally had a good night's sleep, which she'd been desperately needing ever since she'd arrived in Montreal.

She was at the hospital again bright and early with Dr. LaCroix, ready to tackle the angioplasty procedure. After she scrubbed in, she headed into the operating room where Marguerite was waiting. Emile was nowhere to be found, which was a bit strange.

"Good morning, Marguerite. How are you feeling this morning?" Chloé asked brightly.

"Tired," Marguerite replied. "A wee bit nervous."

Chloé leaned over her. "We're going to give you something to relax you, but really this procedure is routine."

"I was married to a surgeon for many years. I know routine doesn't mean safe," Marguerite corrected.

Chloé winked. "You caught me on that one."

Marguerite chuckled softly. "It's okay, *ma chouette*. I understand the risks. Doctor LaCroix explained them."

"Good. I'm glad. So, we're going to get this angioplasty over and done with, then you can recover in your room for a couple of days. I'll make sure Emile visits you more than once."

Marguerite laughed again. "That, *ma chouette*, would be a miracle. Though he did come to see me this morning."

"He did?"

Marguerite nodded. "At five. He woke me up, but I was glad to see him."

"I'm sure you were." Chloé was glad he'd been there; she'd assumed he hadn't visited yet. It pleased her to know that he wasn't so cold to everyone.

"Well," Marguerite sighed. "I'm ready."

"I do have to ask one thing," Chloé said. "Isn't *chouette* an owl?"

Marguerite smiled. "It's a form of endearment. Besides, I do adore owls and you are quite the pretty one."

Chloé's heart melted at her sweet words. "Well, you're my owl, too."

"Doctor MacDonald, are we ready?" the anesthesiologist asked.

"Yes, inject the propofol please and then we'll start the procedure," Chloé instructed.

"Yes, Doctor MacDonald," the anesthesiologist responded.

While the medication was taking effect, Chloé

went over her instruments, and Dr. LaCroix readied the fluoroscopy so they could watch blood flow. When Marguerite was finally sedated enough, the anesthesiologist injected a numbing agent into Marguerite's upper thigh. Then Chloé made the tiny incision to access the arteries and insert the instruments to guide her to the blockages.

There were a few places where the plaque had built up enough to block some of her peripheral arteries. No doubt they were causing numbness in her legs, and if left untreated could lead to gangrene. Using the balloon through the catheter, Chloé was able to clear the plaque and increase blood flow.

There was a large blockage near Marguerite's heart that took several attempts to clear. Once Chloé had managed it, she then inserted a mesh stent to keep the artery from narrowing again. As she placed the stent she looked up into the gallery, where a few medical students had been watching, and she saw Emile.

At first, she didn't recognize him, because he wasn't dressed in his business attire or his white lab coat. He was wearing a blue sweater, which brought out the color of his eyes in contrast to his dark hair. He was staring down at the procedure intently and she could see the concern in his face. It was almost human. Almost like the man she once knew, the man she'd fallen in love with.

The man who broke up with you. The man who said he never wanted a family, remember?

Chloé ignored that logical thought. Right now all she saw was a concerned son.

She smiled up at him. When their gazes locked, even though he couldn't see her mouth from behind her mask, he did return that smile. A tender look could so easily have made her melt, but she had to focus on finishing the procedure.

After placing the final stent, she removed the catheter and had Dr. LaCroix close the small incision. As the nurses and Dr. LaCroix got Marguerite ready to move to recovery, Chloé sent a thumbs-up to the gallery and left the operating room to scrub out.

By the time she was finished, Emile was outside the scrub room waiting for her.

"How did it go?" he asked, his arms crossed. She couldn't help but stare at his muscular forearms, just for a moment.

"Textbook. You watched it."

"I did." He swallowed hard. "I couldn't sleep last night. I was worried about her."

"Of course, she's your mother."

"My father never let these things affect him," he groused.

"Do you know that for sure?" Chloé asked tentatively.

"I do. He wasn't the warmest man. My maman always said I was like him."

Chloé could detect a bit of bitterness in his voice as he said that, and she reached out and squeezed his shoulder. "Hey, it's okay."

"What is?" he asked.

"Whatever it is you're feeling."

Emile took a step back, his spine stiffening, and it was like she could visibly see his wall going back up again. "I'm feeling gratitude toward you for doing that procedure for me."

"I'm glad. I'll go check on her later." Chloé walked away from him. There were times she thought Emile might open up to her, share what he was feeling with her, but then there were times he closed himself off.

She should just put distance between them on her part, too.

It wasn't as though they were romantically linked anymore. They couldn't be. They wanted vastly different things. She shouldn't really be bothered by it.

But she was.

Nuka, you're asking for trouble.

CHAPTER EIGHT

A couple of days later

HONESTLY, EMILE HAD thought that Chloé might actually back out of taking his mother home to Beaupré. After their brief discussion outside the scrub room, he'd barely spoken to her since. He'd see her passing in the halls or in Céline's room, but it had been all business between them.

Every time he saw Chloé interact with a patient, it just melted his heart a little bit, but it also reminded him to give her the distance. When he had listened to her talk to his mother, when he'd watched her do the angioplasty, it had been hard for him not to let all his old emotions surface again. To think about how much he'd been in love with her.

It was a losing battle.

It was impossible not to be enchanted by Chloé. All his staff adored her. A lightness had descended upon the cardio wing and it was all her.

Watching her click so instantly with Marguerite had also triggered a bit of guilt, because he hadn't really connected much with his mother. He was always so annoyed when she said he was like his father, but in that way she was right.

It was funny; he'd used to think being compared

to his father would be a compliment, something that would make him happy, but it really didn't.

That alone was making him question a lot of things, things he wasn't ready to deal with.

Nothing in his life was going to change. How could it? If he'd distanced himself from even his own mother for the past couple of years, how could he possibly entertain the notion of having more with someone like Chloé? Someone so warm and open? Someone who dreamed of a real, happy family?

He couldn't. She deserved to have everything she ever wanted and those were the things he just couldn't give her.

Why not?

Emile ignored that niggling thought, yet again. It had seemed to creep up more and more in his mind since she'd come to Montreal. It was testing his resolve.

Making the past three hours trapped in a car with her even harder.

But it was also nice to have Chloé there, chatting and spreading sunshine. It had been far too long since Emile had an enjoyable car ride like this. His mother's surgery had been no picnic, but now it was a gorgeous day for a trip. Chloé and his mother talked, mostly about art and other things. It was nothing too deep, but Emile could see that his mother was enjoying herself.

It made time pass quickly.

"Oh wow!" Chloé gasped from the backseat.

"What?" Emile asked.

"I think she's looking at the falls, Emile," Marguerite answered. "You should pull in to the turnoff. I wouldn't mind the small break to stretch my legs."

"Very well." Emile merged into the correct lane and took the turnoff for the Montmorency Falls. He hadn't been planning to play tourist today. His plan was to get his mother home to Beaupré, get the nurse he'd hired set up, then head straight back to Montreal. But now he thought it might be nice to visit the falls. He couldn't remember the last time he had seen them.

He paid for parking and they all took the short walk from the parking lot to the area with a view of the water. The roar got louder the closer they approached. Marguerite was moving a bit slowly and sat down on a bench instead of climbing up to the viewing platform.

"Are you okay, Maman? Shall I stay with you?" Emile asked.

"You two go, get closer and see if you can spot the white lady," Marguerite insisted.

"We'll be back soon." Emile kissed the top of his mother's head.

Chloé was snapping a picture with her phone. "White lady?"

Emile rolled his eyes and smiled. "It's a legend of a woman named Mathilde and her betrothed, Louis."

"Really, that's all you're going to tell me?" she asked sarcastically as they made their way up the steps closer to the falls.

"I can give you scientific facts. Montmorency is taller than Niagara."

"That is interesting," she agreed, but sounded bored. "Now, tell me the ghost story."

Emile groaned. "Don't tell me you're into that nonsense?"

"Sure. It's romantic, I assume, unless Louis threw her off the ledge or something?" They stopped at the edge of the platform after climbing up the steps.

"No, he didn't throw her over the edge."

The mist was causing Chloé's hair to curl. It was kind of hot and humid out, so it was nice to have the cool rush of water fanning their faces. Chloé closed her eyes and sighed.

"What was the sigh for?"

"Just enjoying it. It's beautiful," she murmured.

"*Bonne.* I'm glad." And Emile was enjoying it, too. He relaxed for a moment, then remembered he had to keep his wits about him. Last time he'd relaxed around Chloé, he'd kissed her. And now, as he watched her with her eyes closed enjoying the spray of the roaring falls, he desperately wanted to kiss her again.

"So," she said, spinning around to face him. "This white lady story. Tell me about it? Are you hesitating because it's a murder mystery or something?"

"I told you he didn't murder his wife."

"So then why the delay?"

"I can't quite remember all the details. But Louis and Mathilde were set to marry when the British invaded. Louis joined the militia and was killed.

Mathilde was so distraught she donned her wedding dress and threw herself into the falls. Legend is you can see her falling."

"Oh, that is tragic." Chloé turned and squinted. "I can see a rainbow, but no star-crossed lovers."

"You sound disappointed in that."

"I am. I one hundred percent believe in the supernatural and spirits."

"You do?" he asked in disbelief.

"Why is that so shocking?" There was a hint of amusement in her voice. "Remember I like death metal."

"You're a surgeon. A woman of science…"

"So? It's not all just about facts. It's about beliefs." Then she reached out and placed her hand on his chest. "About what's in your heart, Emile."

His body reacted to her delicate hand on his chest, the mist in the air, the warm breeze. It made his heart beat just a bit faster. Even the talk about nonsensical legends was making him forget about the barriers he put up. It was just so easy being with her, talking and joking around. He gazed down into her dark eyes, staring at her long, dark lashes, her slightly parted luscious lips, and fought the urge to kiss her.

Instead, he reached out and tenderly brushed away a strand of her hair. Her cheeks turned pink, and she quickly removed her hand.

"We better get your mother home," she said. "I know it's warm, but I don't want her to catch a chill with all this mist in the air." Then she was rushing past him and down the stairs, breaking the spell.

Which was a good thing.

He had to remember that.

They got his mother settled back into the car and continued down the highway. The chatting had slowed down as his mother was resting, her face rather flushed. Emile was worried that the stop at Montmorency had been a little bit too taxing for her.

It was lunch time when they pulled into Beaupré. His mother's home was a little chalet, painted blue, that sat across from the river. The yard was overgrown with hostas and other blooming wildflowers. What had been a white picket fence the last time Emile was here had been painted over in rainbow colors. It was definitely the home of an artist.

Once they got his mother settled inside and in her bed, Chloé took her temperature.

"Fever?" Emile asked from the doorway, hovering.

"Mild one. I saw there's a hospital in Beaupré, which is good. Do you know any doctors there, maybe a nurse we can hire to check in on her later?"

Emile nodded. "I do. I already arranged that."

"He's very efficient, my Emile," Marguerite responded drowsily.

"Well, I'm still going to give you some Tylenol and I'm not leaving until your fever breaks," Chloé warned. "Even if I have to take the train home."

Marguerite chuckled as Emile groaned. "I won't leave, either," he stated.

"Well, I'm glad to hear it," Marguerite said. "You better not abandon *ma chouette*."

Chloé shared a tender look with him and then placed a cold, wet cloth on Marguerite's forehead. "You need to rest."

She administered some Tylenol and made Marguerite comfortable while Emile called his friend about the arrangements. The nurse he had hired to check on his mother next week would stop by later tonight instead, and Emile was hoping the fever would break before then so he and Chloé could get back to Montreal at a decent time.

When he finished his call, he found Chloé wandering in his mother's front room, staring at all his mother's paintings on the wall, including one small portrait she'd done of Emile. There were also several photographs on the mantel of their times together in the country. Those happy memories that he clung to when he was younger. The summers he'd gotten to spend with his maman were the favorite he'd ever had.

He hadn't thought of them in years. And the last time he spent a summer here had been so long ago now.

"You were cute as a kid," Chloé remarked. "Such chubby cheeks."

He laughed softly. "Yes, well, I seem to have outgrown my baby-fat era."

"Indeed. Don't worry, I had very chubby cheeks while..." She trailed off, her energy shifting to sadness again. He was certain that she had been going to mention her sister but had stopped herself.

"You keep doing that," he remarked.

"Doing what?" she asked, absently still staring at the paintings on the wall, but he knew that she wasn't looking at them. She was far away.

"Changing the subject from your sister."

"Ah, you caught that."

"I did, but I also didn't want to pry."

She sighed. "It's okay. I don't know why I don't talk about it more."

"Yes. I didn't know you had a sister."

"A twin, in fact." This time her smile was a bit wobbly. "You've heard of twin-to-twin transfusion syndrome?"

"I have. It's where one twin receives too much blood."

"My sister Immitaq was that unfortunate twin. I have a mild murmur, but Immi suffered with heart problems most of her life." Chloé drifted off again, quiet, her hands wringing together as if she was thinking of something.

He'd never seen her like this, this raw, vulnerable side to her. Instinctually, he just wanted to pull her into his arms and hold her.

He wanted to tell her not to blame herself, but she was a heart surgeon; she would know it wasn't her fault. There was no logic sometimes when it came to emotions. He knew that better than anyone.

All he could do was let her process it out loud to him. All he could do was listen.

And provide distraction, if she needed it. “I think I’m going to walk to the village and get a bite to eat. Would you like to come for a walk? We can bring back my mother her favorite food. By then her fever should be broken and we can head back to Montreal.”

Chloé nodded, her smile brightening. “I would like that.”

Chloé was appreciative that Emile wanted to change the subject. She was still in shock that she had brought up Immitaq to him, but there had been no point in hiding it. For some reason she was feeling Immi’s presence strongly today, although her usual voice in her head was quiet.

A walk would definitely take her mind off it and help her regain control of her emotions. The last thing Emile or Marguerite needed to see was her sad. They had enough on their plates. She could control her own grief. No one else had to be burdened by it.

There was no reason to be sad or bring anyone else down.

After letting Marguerite know where they were going, they headed out. She followed Emile down the road, walking along the river that eventually flowed into the St. Lawrence. The whole rue was tree lined and full of quaint homes, similar to Marguerite’s in some ways but also vastly different.

It was a short jaunt to the neighborhood *boulangerie*. Chloé’s stomach growled at the smells that were wafting through the open doors from people who came and went.

It was so crowded in there, Chloé sat outside while Emile ducked in and made the order. It wasn't long before he had a bag filled with fresh bread and some sandwiches.

"That smells so good," she remarked as they strolled back to the house.

"It does. It's my mother's favorite place. I haven't been here since I was a kid."

"I'm surprised you stayed in Montreal and didn't stay with your mother."

He shrugged. "I was going to school in Montreal and she didn't want to pull me out. That and my father had more sway and won custody."

"That must have been so hard."

"It was," he said stiffly.

"Well, I thankfully didn't have to deal with that. Custody battles and the like. Just a lot of relatives. I'm practically related to most of the village I came from or at least, they're all involved in our business."

He chuckled. "I don't know what that's like."

"Intrusive," she groused and it made them both laugh. "I'm sorry you had such a hard childhood. You never mentioned it when we were together."

"You can't put all that blame on me. You never told me about your sister or your large intrusive family. I had no idea you were a twin."

"Touché. I guess I can't really complain about that. We didn't really talk much about our personal lives now that I think about it. What did we talk about when we were together?"

"Sex?" he teased, winking at her, which made the butterflies in her stomach do a little backflip.

Her cheeks heated and she nudged him slightly. "Besides that."

"Work, mostly. We were residents in a busy Toronto hospital. We had charting and rounding. We were trying to get all the experience we could so we could make our dreams come true."

"So our relationship back then was superficial?"

His eyes widened. "I didn't think so. I was in love with you."

It came out so quick. He looked a bit stunned at himself.

The admission caught her off guard, too. It shouldn't, though, because she'd been in love with him, too, all those years ago. They'd just never verbalized it before.

Actually, there were times when she wondered whether she ever had fallen out of love with him. The few times she'd gotten involved with someone else, it hadn't lasted long. She'd always blamed it on her commitment to her work, but now she couldn't help but wonder if there was something more there.

There can't be more. Don't get caught up in a romantic ambiance of a quaint Quebec town.

Damn him and his dishy good looks, his French accent and this beautiful place. It was those good looks and accent that had swept her off her feet last time. She did always like the broody heroes.

Back then she'd believed a bit in fairy tales, but that had never been in the cards for her or Emile. And for so long afterward, she really just couldn't see herself having that dream with someone else.

It was just easier to be alone and focus on work.

I was in love with you. That was what he'd said. And while the past tense hurt, it was a good reminder.

"I loved you back then, too," she said. "I guess we were young and dumb. We both had aspirations and dreams and they didn't mesh. I don't regret our time together."

They'd stopped in front of his mother's house, and there was a moment when their gazes locked. Chloé realized that her heart was racing and her body trembled in anticipation of something that she wasn't going to let happen.

She couldn't let it happen. The last kiss had been a mistake. They'd moved on. She couldn't let it happen again.

If she ever did want a family, she had to let Emile go.

"Why is it when we say we're going to be friends, we skirt this dangerous topic?" he asked, chuckling.

"I don't know. I think, in spite of my bright attitude, which drives you nuts, we get along well together." She let out a little breath of relief, glad that it was light again and they weren't talking about love and the heartbreak of when it all ended. Levity was so much easier.

"That is true. Your cheerfulness drove me squirrelly. Always so happy and eager, bleh." He winked and she punched him in the arm. She liked being able to mess around with him again.

"Let's go check on your mother and get back to the city. I need to get some distance from you and your snark," she teased.

"Fine."

They headed back into his mother's house. She left Emile in the kitchen and snuck into Marguerite's room.

She was resting comfortably and opened her eyes slightly when Chloé came in.

"How was your walk, *ma chouette*?"

"Pleasant, or *bonne* as you might say. We brought you some lunch, but I just want to check your temperature. If you're fever-free, I'll bring you some food. Then after we eat, we'll head back to the city."

Marguerite sighed. "I wish you could both stay. It's nice to have the company."

Chloé smiled and took her hand. "I wish I could, too, but there's a little girl in Montreal with heart cancer that I was brought in to treat. I have to check on her."

"I understand. That is important."

Chloé used the digital thermometer and found that Marguerite's temperature had returned to normal. "That's good. You're fever-free. Emile has hired a nurse to check on you. No heavy lifting for ten days. I don't want you to hurt your small incision, but you can walk around and rest when you need to. I'll be back within the week to check on you."

"That sounds good." Marguerite closed her eyes and Chloé slipped from the room as Emile brought a tray with a sandwich and a small pastry.

"How is she?" he asked.

"Her temperature's normal. No fever."

"Good. I left you something to eat in the kitchen."

"Thank you."

Emile slipped past her into his mother's room and she sighed. There was a part of her that wished they could stay here, too.

Emile seemed so comfortable here. Probably because he was out of the shadow of his late father's legacy. Here, he didn't seem so closed off or guarded. Here, it was like he was his real self, just like the man she thought she used to know.

The one she missed the most.

The car ride back to Montreal was silent. Chloé was mulling things over in her head and trying to battle a bunch of emotions. She was also still grappling with the realization that she told him about Immitaq.

Usually, they didn't talk much about Immi in her family, because it always made her parents get maudlin. Luckily, Chloé had always been right there to make them happy again. Making jokes eased the tension.

Immitaq had always been a delight to her parents. Chloé had had to work hard to be like her sister, to bring them some of the joy that Immi's absence had snatched away. It was her duty, just as saving lives was her duty now. If they hadn't been twins, if there had been more specialty care for twin-to-twin transfusion syndrome available, Immi would still be here.

A tear slipped from her eye and she brushed it away quickly, hoping that Emile didn't see it. That was something else she had learned not to do—cry in front of others. She was so glad he hadn't pressed her on the topic.

"That's it." Emile turned on his blinker.

"What?" Chloé asked, shocked.

"Well, we're in Quebec City. It's three o'clock and I think you need to see it. I know we said we weren't, but we're here. Unless you really want to get back to Montreal."

"And if I did really want to go back to Montreal?"

"It doesn't matter. I'm making a decision and we're going to Quebec City."

Chloé laughed, startled out of her moment of sadness by his unprecedented behavior. "Okay, you're the boss."

He nodded. "That's right. We're going to walk around the *Chateau Frontenac*, then we're going to go down to the old part of the city and find a quaint little bistro to have dinner. Maybe ride the *funiculaire*, or walk the *Plains d'Abraham*."

"Whoa, you've got this all figured out, eh?" she teased.

"Not really. Usually, I do like things planned, but we're going to wing it. No reservation, just fun."

"Okay. I like that."

"There's a hint of nervousness in your voice."

"Is there?"

"Just a bit. Trust me, it'll be okay. I know my way around *Petit-Champlain*."

"And where's that?"

"The old part of the city, below the chateau."

"Sounds good. I guess I have nothing to do but trust you." And she was tentatively excited about the prospect. Despite always thinking of herself as such a cheery person, she couldn't actually remember the last time she'd let loose and just thrown caution to the wind. The last time had definitely been with Emile, but that time it had been her instigating it.

"Why are we getting on a ferry?" he complained.

She grabbed his arm. "We're going to the Toronto Islands!"

"I understand that, but why?"

"It's our day off?"

"Why are you saying that in the form of a question?" He frowned and crossed his arms.

"Because you didn't seem to understand that it's our day off, it's a warm summer's day and there's a nude beach on the island."

One of his eyebrows quirked upward. "Are you saying you want to go nude bathing?"

"I am." She grinned.

"Well, then." He rushed forward and scooped her up in his arms, flinging her over the shoulder and carrying her toward Queens Quay. "Let's go!"

"You're smiling again. That's good. What were you thinking about?" Emile asked.

"That trip to the Toronto Islands."

His brow furrowed and then he laughed. "I forgot about that. The skinny-dipping incident."

"Well, it's technically not skinny-dipping when it's an adult nude beach. And you didn't even take off your shorts."

"I remember you did, though."

"Heck, yeah. It was a hot day and I was there to swim. You can't swim in my hometown unless it's an indoor pool. No one swims in the water off Baffin Island unless you're swimming for your life."

"I can imagine. Well, there's no nude bathing in the city."

"That's okay. I haven't prepared myself properly. Things have to be waxed and prepped. Some bits wobble now that I'm older."

Emile sent her a look of disbelief that made her laugh.

He navigated his way to a parking place above the *Petit-Champlain* area. They walked along cobbled streets toward the Chateau Frontenac where the staircase headed down to a place steeped in four hundred years of history, pausing to admire the view from the top of the cliff. It was a bright, sunny afternoon and as they approached the railing overlooking the older part of the city, Chloé could see the bends of the St. Lawrence River, the large ships traversing the blue water and the islands connected by bridges. It was similar to Montreal, but also not. It was old European here.

The *Chateau Frontenac* rose high behind them,

with its red brick and green shingled roof, like it was standing guard over the city.

The brightly colored homes and narrow streets below them looked like they'd been pulled straight from the French countryside. It was so out of place in Canada, or the places Chloé had been to, which were all more reminiscent of frontier buildings than this quaint, old-world charm.

"What do you think?" Emile asked.

"It's beautiful." She leaned against the railing, drinking in the air.

"Well, my favorite bookshop is down in the old part of the city and there are many great places to eat."

"Well, let's go to the bookshop and then sit outside to eat and enjoy this nice weather."

Emile nodded. "That sounds like a very good plan indeed."

Without thinking, she held out her hand and he linked his fingers between hers, like it was the most natural thing in the world. It just felt right. It felt like she belonged.

That was always the problem with Emile, why the breakup had been so hard, because when he was gone it felt like a piece of her was missing. She should let go of his hand, but it was comforting to hold it.

Emile led her down what he said were called "the breakneck steps," though there was nothing sinister about them, and they descended into the lower part of Old Quebec. The streets were narrow and the stone buildings were close together. Signs of various shops hung along the street, *patisseries* and coffee shops that had wonderful aromas wafting from them. Every which way Chloé turned her head, there was something new to look at.

Emile didn't let go of her hand and she didn't pull away as the streets were crowded with tourists and locals.

She was used to the Byward Market in Ottawa and Toronto from her days of residency, so the crowds of people didn't faze her, but she really didn't want to get lost here.

"You doing all right?" Emile asked, pulling her closer as they dodged some oblivious tourists.

"Fine."

"Well, not many people frequent this bookshop, save locals and people from Quebec. It's mostly French editions."

"I don't care. I can't wait to see it."

Emile smiled and they stopped at the end of a smaller alleyway where a sign read *Livre Poussiéreux*. He opened the door and a bell rattled above them.

"*Bonjour*," a man said from behind a counter. "Can I help you find anything today?"

Emile spoke with him quickly in French and the man nodded and went back to his task behind the counter.

"What did you say to him?" Chloé asked.

"I told him we were locals." Emile winked. He let go of her hand and they wandered through the antique used bookstore. It was piled high with volumes of dusty tomes, like something out of an old fantasy novel. Books upon books and even one of those rolling iron ladders as the shelves against the back wall reached almost to the ceiling.

At that moment Chloé almost felt like busting out into song from her favorite cartoon princess movies.

Emile had disappeared, but returned with a book tucked under his arm. “Well? What do you think?”

“I think there must be more than *this* provincial life,” she teased, quoting a line from one of the songs.

Emile groaned. “And I’m *la bête*, am I?”

“Could be. What did you get?”

He glanced down at the book. “An old book from a polar explorer who then wrote fictional stories of characters in the north. I loved his books as a child, but my father threw them out when I was in university. I’ve been trying to track them down ever since.”

“A polar explorer?”

“I was always fascinated with the north.”

“Really?” she mocked. “I hadn’t noticed.”

He rolled his eyes. “Come on now.”

“It’s funny how you ended up in the southern part of Canada.”

“My family has been working and running that hospital’s cardiac wing for generations. It’s hard to walk away from a generational expectation.” There was a slight hint of bitterness in his voice.

She softened her joking then, because she couldn’t

even begin to imagine the pressure he felt growing up. There were deep wounds, too, generational scars, that ran deep in her family. Ones that rippled through the fabric of their community still. And then there'd been so much pain after losing Immitaq. But despite all of it, Chloé had really been surrounded by warmth, affection; she'd never lacked love from her family.

For that she was grateful.

"I'm starving," she announced, changing the subject. "Buy your book and let's get something to eat. Walking past all those coffee and pastry shops was too much a temptation for me."

Emile chuckled. "*Oui.* That sounds good."

They paid for his book then he led her out of the small side street back onto the main rue, where there was a little bistro. It was tucked beside an elevator that went on an angle up the side of the cliff.

"The *funiculaire*," he said, pointing to it.

"Can we ride that back up when we're done?"

"*Mais oui.*" He grinned as she clapped her hands in delight.

They ordered a light supper and some freshly ground coffee. Then they sat there, just enjoying the sights and sounds of Quebec City, laughing and talking about nothing in particular. Just like they always had done in the old days.

If this was friendship with him, Chloé could be happy.

Can you?

When they finished their early dinner, they

walked hand in hand to the *funiculaire* and got their own little elevator to ride back up the cliff, slowly, overlooking the charming lower city and the St. Lawrence River.

"Your home province is very beautiful," Chloé sighed. "I can see why you love it."

"I do love it. But I have always wanted to go to Nunavut. Tell me about it."

"Tell you about it?" she asked. "You never wanted to know before."

"Well, it's clear we didn't really talk about much. So..." Emile nodded and leaned closer. "I want to know. And not the facts about populations and infrastructure. I don't want to hear about the things that you have to tell bureaucrats and politicians. I want to see it through your eyes."

The way he said that to her, so low and husky, made her pulse quicken. He was asking her to describe the place she loved most of all in a deep and intimate way. One she hadn't shared with anyone else.

Usually, when people asked her about the north it was about: *What can we do there? Where can we eat or stay? What are the activities and the history?* Touristy things. In meetings, it was about funding, lodging and trying to attract medical professionals up there.

She was always trying to sell the place. And she got the hint that Emile didn't want to be sold on Nunavut; he wanted to see it through her eyes. It touched her very deeply.

"Well, it's like nowhere else on earth. No, there's no lush greenery where I come from, but the rock and the ice, it's stunning. But in the summer out on the land the lichen, moss, berries like Crowfoot and the purple saxifrage. It blooms in color. Everyone thinks the tundra is a barren wasteland, but there is life there. In the autumn, when it gets dark again, the aurora will come out and paint the sky with vibrant colors." She closed her eyes and thought about the last time she'd really taken a moment to view them, to listen to them. "The best thing I love is the sense of community there. You have to rely on one another to survive."

"It sounds wonderful."

She nodded. "It is."

Their gazes met and her pulse began to race as she stared deep into his eyes. She was losing herself again. He leaned closer, then touched her face, running his thumb over her cheek and over her lips. She trembled with anticipation, remembering how his kisses made her feel.

But she couldn't let this happen.

He wants different things. I want things he can't give me.

And she doubted he'd ever change his mind.

Except, she was so weak when it came to him. All she could remember was the good times. How he always felt like home.

He's not, though, Nuka.

It was true. So when his other hand slipped around her waist, she put her hands on his arm.

"Emile," she whispered. "We can't."

He sighed, all the intention leaving his frame. "I know," he agreed, his voice laced with disappointment.

She stepped back. Her body was still thrumming all over with anticipation, angry that she was ignoring what she really wanted.

The *funiculaire* stopped and the doors opened.

Emile looked away and they quickly disembarked so the passengers that were waiting to descend could board.

They didn't say much as they walked quickly back to where they parked, but she could feel the tension in the air.

That had been far too close a call. She couldn't let it happen again.

Her time with Emile had an end date. When Céline's case was over, Chloé would head back to her work between Ottawa and Iqaluit and he'd stay in Montreal. She hadn't managed to change him all those years ago. There was no way she could now.

And even if she could change him, she couldn't change the world. There was too much work still to be done for her to be thinking about happily-ever-afters with anyone, least of all Emile. There were so many people like Immi out there who needed her.

What about what I need?

She pushed the thought away, furious that she'd let it in. It was selfish and she was satisfied with the course of her life.

So despite her body's demands, she was *glad* she'd had the strength to push him away.

Are you glad, Nuka? I don't think you are.

"I'm sorry," Emile said when they were away from the crowds. "I got carried away."

"So did I," she said, relieved that he'd been the one to bring it up. "We can't let that happen again. I don't want any weirdness between us when we go to do Céline's surgery. What we have now is nice."

He nodded. "Agreed."

They stood there for a few moments longer. God, she hated awkward silences.

"So, should we head back?"

"*Oui.* We better get going."

"Thank you again for showing me around Quebec City and your mother's town. I did have an amazing day."

Emile smiled at her but the smile didn't reach his eyes the same way it did before. "I am glad."

They headed back to his car, still silent. The spell that had been woven over them was broken. Now they were worlds apart in the same country.

It was for the best. Maybe it wasn't fair, but life wasn't fair.

Chloé knew that. As much as she'd loved fairy tales when she was younger, sometimes there just couldn't be a happily-ever-after for everyone.

Sometimes, for some people, there was only an ever-after.

And she was one of them.

CHAPTER NINE

Two weeks later

CHLOÉ WAS FEELING so much more confident about driving around Quebec, that when she went back to Beaupré to check on Emile's mother, she was able to manage it herself. Marguerite's doctor insisted that he could do the check-in, but Chloé had made a promise to Marguerite.

She'd barely seen Emile since Quebec City.

They'd passed each other in the hallways and had a couple of quick meetings about Céline, but that was it. At least there was good news about Céline, who was doing very well on the new course of her chemotherapy; the latest scan looked promising and the tumor was shrinking.

It wouldn't be long before Chloé would be able to perform the surgery and remove the tumor. She was planning a meeting to go over the procedure with the surgical staff that would be involved. Due to the size of Céline's heart, the surgery would be tricky and she wanted to make sure that everyone in that operating room knew what they were up against when the time came.

Emile wasn't the only one to blame for the avoidance game that seemed to be transpiring in the halls of Hôpital de Ville-Marie ever since their ill-fated almost-second-kiss in the *funiculaire*. It had taken Chloé a lot of willpower to remind him that they couldn't give in; even now she caught herself replaying the moment in her head, over and over. And the less she saw of him now, the easier it was to stick to her resolution.

She'd done the right thing in the moment; she had no doubt of it. Only now they weren't really speaking beyond work. And the truth of the matter was she missed him.

She might not be able to have a romantic relationship with him again, but she did miss the camaraderie and the rapport.

And she didn't want to fly up to the remote community of Aivik Bay on Hudson's Bay crammed in a small bush plane with someone she wasn't talking to, because it would be 100 percent awkward.

She picked up the list of supplies that the hospital provided for the community. There was a nurse practitioner up there, and specialists often flew in for checks, especially in good weather. If there was something serious, that specialist could make the suggestion that the patient be flown down to the city. It was similar to the setup Chloé currently had with Iqaluit.

She went through the notes that had been sent over and read reports from the nurse practitioner, who mentioned a few causes for concern with respect to cardio patients who needed assessment about possible surgery. That would be where she and Emile came in. They could assess and deem if it was necessary.

If they could keep their heads on straight and act normal.

Or normal-*ish*.

She set down the list and took a sip of her coffee. It was four in the morning and their flight was leaving at six with the estimated time of arrival of seven-thirty to get their day started. They weren't going to be leaving Aivik Bay until nine at night. It was going to be a long, long day. And she'd made sure that her own supplies consisted of a small overnight bag, just in case they got stuck up there. She'd learned that when traveling to remote communities, it was always best to be prepared.

"Are the supplies almost loaded into the transport to the airport?" Emile asked, coming into her office. He was dressed in jeans and a polo shirt with a light but warm jacket, but she didn't see a duffel or a knapsack. Only a leather messenger bag that looked too nice to travel up north. Actually, it looked like it hadn't been much of anywhere.

"Is this your first time doing a round up north?" she asked carefully.

"*Oui.* Why?"

"You don't have an overnight bag." She nodded in the direction of the messenger bag.

He cocked an eyebrow. "Why would I need an overnight bag? We're just going for the day."

"Something could happen."

"It's summer. I doubt there will be a snowstorm."

She narrowed her eyes. "How very stereotypical of you. You know, even though where we're going is above the tree line, it's farther south than Yellowknife and it's summer."

"But Yellowknife has trees!" Emile stated, all proud of himself.

"Yes, but…the tree line in your lovely province ends at the fifty-sixth parallel and not above sixty."

Emile blinked a couple of times. "Why are we discussing parallels and tree lines?"

"Because you seem to think it's snowing where we're going and it's not. Plus, making assumptions."

"I never said it was snowing." Emile scrubbed a hand over his face. "Why are we talking about snowing? It's summer and I don't know what could possibly waylay us. We're going up for a day. I don't need an overnight bag."

"Okay, suit yourself." Chloé took another sip of her black coffee. "Look, I think we need to talk more about what happened a couple of weeks ago on the elevator thing."

"The *funiculaire*," he corrected.

"Now who's being pedantic?" She smiled slightly.

"My apologies. What about it?"

"We've been avoiding each other. I say *we* because I'm just as much to blame."

"I've been busy," Emile stated. "But I do see your point."

"I don't want our trip up to Aivik Bay to be weird. I like working with you. When we do Céline's surgery at the end of the month we need to work together seamlessly. So no weirdness. We've got to move past it, all of it."

Emile sighed. "You're right. We do and I'm sorry that I've been avoiding you."

"You are not the only one to blame in that, *ma chouette*. Like I said, I was avoiding you, too."

He cocked an eyebrow. "Owl?"

"Not appropriate? Rats. I thought it was a friendly endearment."

"Not for me," he snickered. "I agree, though. We'll move on and just forget about it."

"That's all I ask."

She picked up her overnight bag and they walked together to the waiting transport.

It was a slightly rough ride from the hospital to the airport in the transport van to where the charter planes were. Chloé was used to riding on bush planes, but she saw Emile frown when he watched as a tiny Cessna with floats was being loaded with the supplies and he realized that was how they were getting north to Aivik Bay.

"You look a little green," Chloé teased gently.

"I've never flown on a small plane like this. I mean, I've read about them."

"It'll be okay. I've flown on worse-looking planes in my life. Think of it as an adventure, something you've always wanted."

He nodded. "You're right."

"Good."

Once everything was loaded, they boarded the plane, put on their noise-canceling headphones and the engines roared to life. Chloé sat across from Emile, their knees almost touching in the small enclosed space as the plane taxied on the runway then took to the sky.

When they were in the air, she just relaxed and enjoyed watching the scenery through the window. The city gave way to rolling hills and countryside, which then turned into boreal forest with flowing rivers. Before long, the tree line disappeared and she could see Hudson's Bay like a big blue shimmering sheet north of them.

The plane finally made its descent toward a sandy beach at the edge of the bay and Chloé could see the familiar sight of a remote northern community clustered together. There were boats on the water and dirt roads that connected the homes. The rocks outside town were blooming with purples and greens. Metal modular homes, some painted in vibrant colors and others in that familiar shade of bright green, dotted the landscape. There were solar panels, trying to soak up and take advantage of the longer hours of daylight this far north. As they got closer, she could see kids on their bikes, racing toward the airport at the edge of the community, wondering who or what was coming into town. Up on a hill she could see a white picket fence marked by white crosses, a typical cemetery. All the communities were so different, yet they were also the same, with the rugged land of the north connecting them all.

"Welcome to Aivik Bay," the pilot said over the radio. "We'll be making our landing in five minutes. Tray tables up!"

Chloé laughed at the sarcasm. She leaned over and tapped Emile on the knee. "What do you think?"

He nodded. "It's just how I pictured it from the books I read as a child, but better."

"And first bush plane ride?"

"Fine." He smiled, but it was a little strained.

She gave him a silly and encouraging thumbs-up, which made him groan, but he relaxed and this time when there was a twitch of a smile, it was genuine and not forced.

The thought of him being happy with a northern community actually gave her a sense of pride, because she always did love her home, where she came from.

Nuka, maybe he'll move north with you? Maybe it doesn't have to be so black-and-white?

Chloé shook Immi's voice away.

There was no time to entertain a notion like that. She'd closed that chapter. And she had work to focus on. She was going to show Emile the north and how worthwhile it was to give yourself to something greater and make your own legacy.

Whether he would listen or not, that was up for debate. Emile had always stated Montreal was his legacy. No family, head surgeon. He'd done those things. She doubted he'd change now. He was so stubborn in that regard.

* * *

Emile hated that he'd been avoiding Chloé since Quebec City, but the truth of the matter was he couldn't stop thinking about her. When she was with his mother, she'd been so sympathetic and gracious. She hadn't even chastised him for not visiting Marguerite. He'd been grateful—he was busy enough doing that inwardly himself.

Emile knew she'd gone down to Beaupré again to do the checkup, because since the health scare, he'd been checking in with his mother more. And he'd been enjoying it.

Pieces of himself he'd locked away in order to carry out his father's legacy were bubbling up to the surface. Being with Chloé in Quebec City, laughing and enjoying a tranquil moment, had just reminded him of something better.

He hadn't meant for their near-kiss to happen. He wasn't sure what had come over him, but he had been utterly lost in the memory of the softness of her lips.

Even though he'd known it was wrong, a bad idea, he just hadn't been able to keep himself from slipping his arm around her waist. Only when she'd stepped away had he come back down to reality and realized his mistake.

Chloé didn't want him. And that was okay. It hurt, but he shouldn't be surprised. They'd always wanted different things in life. Things he couldn't give her. He didn't want to ruin that dream for her.

If having her in his life in this professional capacity was how it had to be, then so be it.

It was for the best, and that was what he had to keep reminding himself.

When they got off the plane, they were greeted by a crowd of people, but a red-headed woman with a knitted cap and a smattering of freckles stepped out of the throng to welcome them.

"Doctor MacDonald and Doctor Moreau, I'm Janet Hobbes and I'm the registered nurse in Aivik Bay. Thank you for coming up here. There's a couple of outlying communities that are sending patients in by boat once they heard you were here today. We have a small clinic/hospital here in Aivik Bay to work with and these other communities are part of our catchment. I only mention it because they weren't in my initial report."

"The pleasure is ours," Emile stated. "We brought supplies as well from Hôpital de Ville-Marie."

"Excellent," Janet said excitedly. "Hey, Jerry and Carl," she called to two men, "get the quads ready and take the supplies being offloaded to the clinic, yeah?"

"Yeah, yeah," one of the two said, waving. "We've got you, Janet."

"It's a short walk," Janet stated. "I hope you don't mind. There's not a whole lot of vehicles around here, although there's hopefully going to be a ship making its round with cargo in a couple of weeks."

"It's not a problem," Chloé stated. "I get it can be hard to get vehicles up here. I'm from a small community on Hudson's Bay originally and now my family is in Iqaluit."

Janet beamed. "I did wonder. Your tattoos are a giveaway."

Emile followed behind Chloé and Janet as they chatted. Behind him, some kids were following along laughing. He glanced back over his shoulder and they all froze, eyes wide.

If he was his father, he'd just ignore them, but then again, his father would never have come here. So instead, Emile smiled and winked, making the gaggle of children laugh.

It warmed his heart to see them so happy. He remembered those days when he hadn't had a care in this world.

It actually made him feel a little lonely, thinking of the life he'd never have.

The family he'd never have.

"We don't get a ton of visitors here," Janet remarked, spying the children.

"I gathered," Emile stated. "It's fine."

"Here's the clinic. The first patient that needs to be seen by a heart specialist is coming at eight, I think, and then it's a fairly steady stream. I'm so glad there are two of you. I hope this will be okay? It's a long day. Also, I may still need to see emergency patients. This is, in fact, our hospital, too."

"Don't worry about that," Chloé stated.

"You're sure it's okay? Some visiting doctors get weird," Janet said.

"More than okay," Emile reassured. "It's why we're here."

The clinic was a white-and-red building at the edge of town, close to the water, which would be good for those coming by boat. It was built on top of a rock outcropping, but part of it was elevated by stilts because of the permafrost in the ground. They clambered up the steps and Janet opened the door to the clinic, flicking on the lights.

Emile wandered around and peeked in the back. It wasn't big, and there were two exam rooms. He was pleased to see a small ultrasound and X-ray machine. There was also a well-stocked medicine cabinet.

"I'm so looking forward to working with you both today," Janet said. "You can leave your coats and gear in the staff room. A couple of the elders are going to bring lunch and dinner to you both."

"They don't have to do that," Emile said, but he was appreciative.

"No, they want to. Besides, there's no real restaurants in town. Home-cooked catering here."

"That sounds great," Chloé stated.

Emile followed Chloé to the staff room where they stored their gear.

"You ready for this?" she asked. "It sounds like it's going to be a jam-packed day."

"More than ready." And he was. He couldn't remember the last time he was actually excited to do clinical work. For so long he'd been bogged down with the running of his department. He was involved with surgeries, but there he usually knew what to expect.

Today, what would be walking through the door would be the unknown.

Almost like the time he'd done rounds in the emergency room when he was an intern. When he was exposed to all the departments of medicine.

It would be a long day, but this was what he actually loved about being a doctor and he was glad he was here for it. In a way, he was living out a long-standing dream, without having to give up work in Montreal.

It was only a taste, but he'd savor it.

Janet hadn't been kidding when she said the patients would be hitting the clinic like a tidal wave. It wasn't just people from Aivik Bay, but from other smaller communities that were farther up the coast. Emile prescribed medication, and there were a couple of patients he saw who needed surgery, so he was able to fill out the proper requisitions to have them flown down to Montreal as soon as possible, so that he and his staff could do the procedures. Anytime Chloé had one of those requisitions to fill out she sent the patient to him, because she didn't have the authority to refer to Hôpital de Ville-Marie.

They had a brief respite at midday when they were brought a potluck lunch, complete with bannock, which Emile had never tried before. Everything he ate was delicious and very much appreciated.

Eventually, there was a lull and he had a moment

to breathe. He thought he'd try to have a power nap, but found sleep wouldn't come; he was running on endorphins and enjoying remote medicine. Still, it was hard to keep his eyes open.

"Here," Chloé said, coming into the room he'd been hiding in. "I brought you a coffee because you look like you're dragging."

"You made me coffee?" he asked.

"No. Uh, Janet did." Then she looked askance as she took a sip.

Emile was hesitant, but it smelled good. He took a slug and then winced as the bitterest, strongest, *thickest* coffee he'd ever tasted slid down his throat. He cursed. "What is that?"

"Strong coffee," Chloé chuckled. "This stuff will keep you up for a week!"

"No doubt. *Merde*, that's what it tastes like." He took another sip. As much as he wanted to pour it down the drain, he could use the boost to keep going. They still had hours before they got back on the plane to Montreal.

"Do you know what *merde* tastes like then?" she teased, a twinkle in her eyes.

"No, but if I had to guess—this. Why are you drinking it so easily?"

Chloé sat on the edge of the desk he was sitting at. He couldn't help but admire her long legs as she crossed them. As much as he was trying to ignore how close she was, he did remember how nicely they'd once wrapped around him.

This is what got you in trouble the last time.

"I'm used to this stuff," Chloé said. "This is the kind of stuff my *ataata* would brew up when we were at our cabin. Kept you going and in the winter keeps you warm."

"I'll take your word on that." Emile set the mug down, nudging it away.

"Doctors?" Janet said, poking her head in. "We have our next patient. She's…not well. It was a long trip by boat."

"Is she in the waiting room?" Emile asked, standing up.

Janet nodded. "She is."

Both he and Chloé got up and walked out to the waiting room.

The patient was a young girl, maybe no more than thirteen. Her breathing was labored—Emile could hear the raspy gasps for air across the room. She was lying on the floor, her head in her mother's lap.

Chloé's demeanor changed instantly. She froze in her tracks, her eyes locked on the young girl.

"Doctors, this is Immitaq Peever. She's from Kamik, farther north."

As soon as Janet said the name, Emile glanced over at Chloé. She had gone pale and looked like she was staring at a ghost. Immitaq was the name of her twin, he recalled, the one who passed away.

"We heard there were heart surgeons coming here and we decided to make the trip. We couldn't afford a plane trip, but we have a boat…" Immitaq's mother stated.

"There's no need to explain," Emile said, kneeling down. He smiled at Immitaq. "I'm Doctor Moreau. Can I listen to your heart?"

Immitaq nodded. "Okay. Just give me a moment and I can get up."

"No. You stay there." Emile looked up at Chloé. "Can you pass me a stethoscope?"

"Yes," Chloé stammered. She handed Emile a stethoscope and then knelt down on the other side of Immitaq, helping her mother to raise the girl up so that Emile could listen to her heart from her back.

He frowned as he heard the beat. It was quick, like there was a blockage, but there was no way to get an angiogram done here, if that was what she needed. At least there was an ultrasound so he could take a look at her heart.

"I would like to do an ultrasound of your heart, so we're going to have to get you up and into an exam room."

"Her father can carry her, but he's down on the beach," Mrs. Peever stated.

"I can carry her. If that's okay with you, Immitaq?" Emile asked.

"Yes." Immitaq nodded.

Emile stood and then reached down to scoop the young girl into his arms. She was light and it was clear she was losing weight, but there was swelling in her face, so she was retaining fluid. Chloé went ahead of them and got the exam room and ultrasound ready. Emile laid the girl on the bed.

"I'm going to step out and Doctor MacDonald and your mom are going to help you get into a hospital gown. Doctor MacDonald is going to do the ultrasound of your heart and I'm going to watch the monitor."

Immitaq nodded. "Okay."

Emile stepped out of the room and waited until he was called back in. Chloé was still a bit subdued, but she was chatting to the patient and her mother while she got out the ultrasound jelly. Emile turned off the lights and they turned on the ultrasound.

"This will be cold, Immitaq," Chloe remarked as she spread the gel and then placed the probe. She was watching the screen along with Emile. "Can you hold your breath?"

Immitaq held her breath.

Emile could see there was a blockage, but there wasn't anything they could do about it up here. Immitaq had to get down to Montreal and have an angioplasty.

They finished with the ultrasound and then Emile pulled Chloé out of the room. "She needs to take our plane," he stated. "I need to get her to Montreal and another surgeon can do the angioplasty."

"Do you think she'll make it there?" Chloé asked. "She's showing signs of a blood clot."

"They have the medication to set up a thrombolytic therapy. We can get her an IV and then transport her down on the plane with her parents. It's a short flight."

Chloé chewed on her bottom lip. "It's worth a shot. It's a good plan, but it means we're stuck here overnight. I doubt they'll get another plane up here in time."

Emile sighed and then shrugged. "It is what it is. I can sleep in these clothes."

A soft smile hovered on Chloé's face, her eyes full of tears. "See, you tempted fate with that fancy messenger bag."

He rolled his eyes. "Let's get this treatment set up. You talk to Immitaq's parents and I'll make the arrangements for the flight and her being received in Montreal."

Chloé nodded. "Okay. And then we'll finish out our day. I get the sofa in the staff room."

He just chuckled and left to make the calls he needed to make while Chloé handled the treatment. Immitaq would have to be on the IV drip for the rest of the day and then she could take their plane this evening.

Emile had no problem getting the staff at Hôpital de Ville-Marie ready for his patient. Dr. LaCroix would wait and arrange everything with the surgeons on duty.

Janet was very helpful setting up the IV and getting Immitaq comfortable. Once the drip was in place there was nothing more for them to do but continue to see the patients that trickled in as the day waned.

Emile watched the clock, though, waiting for that flight to return. And he could see the concern etched in Chloé's face, too. The ghosts haunting her.

What he wanted to do was take her in his arms

and reassure her that *this* Immitaq would be okay, but he couldn't. Frankly, it was amazing that the girl was alive and he knew that Chloé knew that, too.

When it was finally time for Immitaq to get on the plane, Emile carried her out to the waiting ATV, which had a wagon secured to the back to pull her and her parents to the airport. Once he was sure she was settled, he followed on foot to get the whole family safely on the plane and place the drip in Immitaq's arm.

In fact, he ended up carrying her aboard himself.

"Here you go," he said, gently sitting her down in the plane. He checked the IV was secure, belted her in, then tucked a blanket around her.

"I don't like flying," she said, her voice weak.

"Neither do I, but it's a short flight and you get to see Montreal and the hospital where I work, which has the most amazing children's ward." Emile smiled at her. "Your own television and there's gaming systems. You'll feel better in no time."

Immitaq's eyes lit up and she nodded. "I am excited to see the city."

"I'll come and see you there tomorrow, eh?" Emile said warmly.

"Okay."

Emile climbed out of the plane where Immitaq's father was waiting.

"Thank you, Doctor Moreau, and thank Doctor MacDonald, too, yeah?"

"I will. My staff is prepped for her. You and your wife can stay with Immitaq tonight and then we'll get you both set up with lodging for her post-operative care and recovery."

Mr. Peever nodded and followed his wife on the plane.

Emile gave instructions to the pilot, who said he would return in the morning to bring him and Chloé back down to Montreal. Emile stayed until the plane took off. Watching it leave safely gave him a sense of hopeful relief. When the Peevers made it to the hospital, he would get a call from the staff there and a status update.

As he watched the plane recede into the sky, Emile thought back to the argument he'd had with his father about being too friendly with patients. Now it seemed trivial.

It had been good to have that moment of connection, like a part of him that had been asleep for so long was waking up. This feeling was why he'd become a doctor. In that instant, he felt he understood Chloé a little better and remembered his own dreams about remote medicine. The ones his father had quickly quashed.

Today had been one of the most exhausting and rewarding ones he'd spent as a doctor in a long time. There was a part of him that could see himself here, in a place like Aivik Bay.

I want to stay.

The thought surprised him. How could he walk away from Montreal now? There was too much responsibility waiting for him there.

He swallowed down his doubts, like he always

did, shook his head and headed back to the clinic, eagerly awaiting the call from Dr. LaCroix to let them know the Peevers were all okay.

As he climbed back up the steps, Janet came running up to him. "I have a place for you and Doctor MacDonald to stay," she said breathlessly.

"Oh? I assumed we'd sleep in the clinic."

"Well, you can, but the couch is really uncomfortable. There's a guest lodging. It's small, but the community would like you two to stay there for the night. Everyone is just so grateful for what you and Doctor MacDonald did for the Peevers."

"Well, that would be most agreeable," Emile said, because he didn't relish the idea of sleeping on the floor.

"And dinner will be delivered there. There are no more patients. I can't thank you and Doctor MacDonald enough," Janet gushed.

"Well, I'll have to talk to my board of directors, but I would actually like to make it a quarterly trip if I can. It's too long for some of them to wait at the moment." All he could think about as he spoke was Immitaq, how urgently she'd needed help. What if the premier hadn't asked them to come up here today? Emile shuddered to think of that reality.

Janet's eyes lit up. "That would be amazing."

Emile nodded. "I'll keep you posted."

He headed into the clinic where Chloé was slouched in a waiting-room chair. She looked tired, but there was also a hint of sadness there. And he knew, without a doubt, that everything that had happened with that young girl had her thinking about her sister.

"Chloé?" he asked gently.

She sat up and plastered a wobbly smile on her face. "Oh. Hey."

"You okay?"

"I'm fine."

"You don't..."

"I'm fine!" she insisted, but again, her smile didn't reach her eyes. It was forced, like she was putting on a brave face. And she didn't need to do that with him. "So, am I taking the couch tonight?"

"Janet found us accommodations. So grab your stuff."

"What accommodations?" she asked quizzically.

"A place they offer to visitors as emergency shelter. It's got to be better than that couch."

Chloé laughed softly, perking up. "You're probably right."

They collected up their belongings and followed Janet to a little house in town.

"We use this for visiting elders, but since we have none with us today, the community would like to offer it to you both since you gave up your ride home." Janet opened the door to the home.

"It's not locked?" Emile asked, curious.

"No. We don't lock doors around here. We always offer a place to shelter," Janet explained.

"That's very generous," Chloé said. "To offer us a place to stay."

"It is," Emile agreed.

"There's food waiting for you in the kitchen. Just relax. There's a large solar flare projected tonight so maybe the aurora will come out, but it's weak in the summer. Not much night up here." Janet waved and left.

Chloé walked inside and Emile followed. It was a small home; everything was in one room. A tiny kitchen in the corner, a couch, wood stove and one bed in the corner.

"Still want the sofa?" he teased.

"Nope." She winked. It appeared that she was coming back around. She set her knapsack on the bed and then sat down next to it. "That was a long day."

"It was." He sat down on the couch. "Do you think we'll see the aurora tonight?"

"If you can stay up late enough for it. The sun won't set for a while and when it does, it won't be for long." She started fiddling with her thumbs and he could tell she was lapsing into melancholy again.

"Look, I know that the young girl affected you."

Chloé nodded. "She did. She reminded me of my sister, but I guess you figured that out."

Emile got up and sat next to her. "Tell me about her."

"What is there to tell? She died." She tried another of those horrible forced smiles.

"You always have to put on a brave face?" Emile asked.

"What do you mean?" Chloé asked, her body going rigid.

"You're a sunshine personality, for sure."

"Is that a bad thing?"

"No. But… How do you really feel?"

Chloé stood up and began to pace. "I survived. Immitaq didn't. *My* Immi didn't. And just seeing that young girl with the same name…it was all too much."

"No doubt."

"I try to be happy a lot of the time because it helped my parents. They were so sad… It was the least I could do."

"The least you could do?"

She shrugged. "Sure. I didn't want to burden them. If I was happy then they didn't have to worry about me. I got good grades, made them laugh… It was easier on them."

"What about you?"

"What about me? I lived." She brushed away a tear quickly from her cheek. "If doctors like us had been up there when Immi… She might be still alive."

Emile stood up and pulled Chloé into his arms and she sobbed a bit, clinging to him. "It's okay. I've got you."

"I'm glad," she whispered.

Maybe it was his turn to cheer her up.

"Shall we eat something, maybe go for a walk?" he suggested.

"I would like that."

"Good."

As much as he wanted to stay here and hold her,

he knew that would lead to something else. Something they'd both agreed could never happen, that Chloé had stated plainly that she didn't want.

The truth was no matter what he told himself, Emile did want her. Her humor, her charm, her strength and optimism. Everything he'd never had when he was growing up. He was falling in love with her again, or maybe he never really stopped.

What he was sure of, though, was that she just saw him as a friend. She'd made that clear, so he'd resist holding her, comforting her, even though it was all he really wanted to do.

She deserved to fall in love with someone who could give her everything she wanted. As much as Emile wanted to be the one to do that, he wouldn't risk failing, risk crushing her bright personality and having their love turn to bitterness like his parents' had.

He wouldn't do that to Chloé.

She deserved better than him.

CHAPTER TEN

When Chloé had seen that young girl with the same name as her sister, suffering from a heart disease, she'd frozen. It was like her whole world had gone still. And it had taken all of her strength to keep up a brave face for as long as she had.

Emile had really taken the lead on the whole thing and she was so thankful for that. He'd stepped in, where she faltered.

And it had been so kind of him to offer up their seats in the plane. His softer side, peeking through again.

There was a part of Chloé that wouldn't relax until she knew that the young girl was safe in Montreal and was on her way to recovery. This Immitaq's case was just a reminder about why Chloé did what she did, why she was so passionate about her work. Especially when she thought about the fact that if they hadn't come when they did, Immitaq wouldn't have lived much longer.

Thinking of it like that had saddened her all the more. How many lives had been lost because the right doctors weren't there?

When Emile had pulled her into his arms, she'd known she should step away, but she couldn't. It had felt so good to be comforted and wrapped up in his arms. She could've stayed there forever.

It had been a relief when he'd been the one to break the contact and suggested that walk…but also not so much.

She'd wanted more.

She wanted the physical connection with him. What she didn't know was how she was going to ask for that or what kind of can of worms it would open up. She'd pushed him away in Quebec City. They'd both agreed that it had been the right thing to do.

Only right now she didn't care about the right thing. She just wanted him, and the sense of security he offered. She was being haunted tonight and she needed to chase the ghosts away.

"Come, you need to eat," Emile said as he dished up some of the fish and potatoes that had been provided for them. "It looks good. What kind of fish is it, I wonder?"

"Arctic char," she replied offhandedly. "It's one of my favorites."

"Well, you need to eat something. It's been a long day. You can't just exist on lunch, which was hours ago, and that sludge you call coffee."

Chloé laughed, but it was still laced with some sadness. At least he'd made her laugh. Sort of like she'd always done for her family. It was nice to have someone do that for her. "You don't like camp coffee?"

"No offense to *ataata*, but no." He grinned, handing her a plate.

Chloé sat down at the table across from him. The

food was home cooked and it had been awhile since she'd had it. It was a comfort.

"This is good," Emile remarked.

"Nothing like a fresh catch."

"Agreed. So walk after? Or… When does the sun go down here? Are we too late? It's about nine o'clock."

"Not until near midnight and then maybe sort of dusky. We're nearing the solstice. Longer days for sure."

Emile's eyebrows rose. "Wow."

"You know for someone who reads a book series set in the north…" It was a gentle tease.

"It was a long time ago that I read those, and they were mostly set in the winter, so give me a break."

She chuckled. "Okay, just a small one."

"Thanks."

They shared a smile; that made her heart skip a beat. Companionable silence. It was comforting.

"I want to thank you for the hug. I… It meant a lot." She reached out and took his hand. Emile didn't pull away; instead, he gave her hand a squeeze.

"That's what friends are for."

She nodded slowly. "Right."

They finished their food and then cleaned up the dishes so they could leave them tidy for the elders. Then they headed outside, where the sun was hanging low, but still bright. A perpetual twilight. It reminded Chloé of summers out on the land with her father and with Immi.

Summers were always Immi's favorite. They

would pick berries and make jams. Then Chloé would pick the purple saxifrage and put it in Immitaq's hair.

"What're you thinking about?" Emile asked as they walked down along the beach. The water was calm. There was just a gentle lapping against the sand and the rocks. There were a few fishing boats out on the water still, taking advantage of the longer daylight.

"My sister. She loved summer," Chloé sighed.

"Your sister sounds lovely. It was just me and my father."

"Tell me about him. I only saw him the one time when he came to speak at the hospital and he seemed kind of formidable."

"That is a nice way of saying it," Emile groused. "He didn't show affection. My mother did. Now I think… I think I wish I could've lived with her, but it was impossible. My father had so much more sway."

"I'm surprised he never remarried."

"Me, too," Emile admitted. "Then again, work was his life. It was the reason my parents split up. My father's work came first. Always. And my mother couldn't compete. I like to think that maybe he didn't move on because he still loved her, but then again, I don't know if he really loved anything but the hospital."

"I think he loved you. He must've."

"He never showed it," he said moodily.

"And your mother never remarried."

"Ah, that's because she loved my father. She waited for him to come back and he never did."

Chloé didn't say much, but she thought on that statement. Thinking of Marguerite waiting for her ex-husband to return tugged at her heartstrings.

Was it really work that was keeping Chloé from dating, from having a family, the way she'd always claimed? Or maybe, just maybe, was she just waiting, too?

Waiting for Emile.

"Well, I'm sorry your mother loved and waited."

"So am I. It's why I don't want a family."

"You're still so sure you don't want kids?" she asked.

"No. Not with my work. My childhood was lonely. I won't do that to a child." His expression hardened for a second then he looked at her tenderly. "What about you? You always said…" He trailed off.

"I do want kids…but work…" It was all an excuse. There were so many real reasons. She wanted love and marriage, but she was still nursing a broken heart from all those years ago. She was afraid of having a child who had problems like Immitaq. And she'd spent so many years dedicated to medicine and to saving people like her sister, that she couldn't selfishly give it up to start a family.

Maybe if she had a partner who was supportive, she wouldn't have to walk away. Maybe she could make it work.

One thing she knew; that partner wouldn't be

Emile. His work always came first. He'd made that clear, even just now.

They didn't say anything further. They just stood there on the beach, staring out over the water.

"What're those?" he asked, pointing.

She turned and saw jets of air and then the white back slip above the surface of the bay and she smiled. "Beluga, I suspect."

"A whale?" he asked, his voice awed.

"Sure, they come up into the Hudson and James Bay all the time in the summer."

"Amazing." They shared a grin.

"You look like a child on Christmas morning," she chuckled.

"It's been a dream of mine for so long to see a wild whale and up north." He whispered those words, the wonder apparent in his voice.

Her heart was beating quickly. She leaned into him and he wrapped his arms around her. She rested her head against his shoulder, just reveling in the feeling of being close to him, because that was all she wanted right now.

She just wanted to be close to him again, even just for one moment. Even if it couldn't happen again, she wanted to be with Emile.

Even though all logic told her she shouldn't.

His phone vibrated. He pulled it out, answered and put it on speaker. "Doctor LaCroix, what's the status?"

"Immitaq Peever had her blockage, the clot, removed. She's stable and Doctor Rosenbaum thinks she'll make a full recovery."

"*Bonne*, keep us posted." Emile ended the call.

Chloé let out a breath of relief. "That's wonderful."

"It is indeed."

"Thank you for supporting me today," she murmured. "It means so much."

"Of course. Thank you for bringing me up here and getting a taste of your world. I had no idea."

"And what do you think?"

"You're doing amazing things. I wish…"

Her breath caught in her throat. "You wish what?"

"It doesn't matter. I'm just glad I'm here with you."

Chloé shivered and she took Emile's hand. "Let's go back. I'm tired."

"Me, too."

They walked slowly back to the cabin. She was trembling with anticipation, because she knew what she wanted to ask him. She wanted to let him know what she needed. And tonight she just needed *him*.

She needed touch and warmth and, above all else, him. She just wanted to be held in his arms and to forget everything else. Forget the pain she buried away; forget that she always had to be the bright light for everyone else.

She just wanted her old Emile, the man she'd never really stopped loving. Deep down she knew it wasn't just geography separating them, but a desire for different things. He didn't want a family and she did, eventually. She couldn't give that up, couldn't give up any of her dreams, but she could have this one night with him.

Once they were inside, she stood there, suddenly so nervous. She hoped he would say yes, but she would understand if he didn't. So much water had passed under the bridge since they'd been together.

"I'll take the couch," he remarked, but he seemed to linger as if he wanted the same thing, too. As if he also felt the magic that was electrifying the air.

"You don't have to." It was barely a whisper.

"Pardon?" he asked.

"You don't have to take the couch. In fact, I would…" Her face heated with a flush.

Emile took a step closer and he brushed his knuckles over her cheek, causing her blood to burn. "You would what?"

"I would like you to kiss me," she murmured.

"You pushed me away last time."

"I know. It was hard to do that."

"Chloé, are you sure?"

She nodded. "Positive."

"I don't know if it's wise."

"I don't think it's very smart, either, but the truth of the matter is I want to be with you, Emile. I know that we can't have forever. We work so far apart and we're on different paths, but I would like one more time. Just one more moment with you."

"I would like that, too," he said, his voice deep and laced with promise. "Only if you're sure."

"I've never been so sure about something in my entire life."

Even though she always put on a brave face, right now she felt completely vulnerable. And she needed that, too. She was tired of being the rock, and her family wasn't around. She needed to feel and let go. She'd opened up a part of herself to Emile, the grief that she didn't share with anyone else. With him she could be free.

Emile had always been her safety net. Most of the time she was putting everyone else first, like she'd done most of her life. Tonight she wanted to be selfish and indulge in the one thing she wanted and could briefly have.

Him.

"Chloé, should we really?"

"Do you not want to?"

"Oh no, *ma chere*. I do. More than you know, but I don't have a condom."

"It's okay. I'm on the pill. This is what I want, Emile. I want to be with you tonight. I want you to make love to me one more time."

She couldn't really believe that one more time would be enough, but it would have to be.

Emile drew her into his arms and kissed her again. Just like he had after their dinner at *Choisir*, down by the river. This was what she'd wanted when they were at the *funiculaire*, but she'd stopped it. Tonight this ride wasn't stopping.

She wrapped her arms around his neck, pressing her body against him. Annoyed that there were so many layers of clothes between them because all she wanted was nothing so he could touch her. Possess her.

Emile's hands slipped under her shirt, cupping her breasts. His hands hot on her exposed skin made her nipples harden, his fingers lightly trailing over her. Then he scooped her up and carried her a couple of steps to the bed, setting her in the middle, where she proceeded to sink into the old mattress.

She screeched with laughter.

"*Merde!* Are you okay?" he asked, humor lacing his voice.

"Yes," she giggled. "It was just unexpected."

He grinned. "Well, I see one more problem with this whole thing."

"And what's that?"

"We're both still dressed," he pointed out, the huskiness in his voice making her heart skip a beat as he pulled off his shirt and she got to drink in the sight of his muscular chest.

Her blood thundered in her ears, her body fizzing with anticipation as she quickly took off her clothes, until nothing was between them.

Emile sat down on the bed, pulling her close, trailing his hands over her body, making her ache for more. He pressed kisses against her neck.

"I remember our first time together like it was yesterday."

"Me, too," she whispered as his kisses traced lower down her body, along her collarbone, over her breasts, his tongue circling her sensitive nipples.

Chloé lay back against the bed, the air crackling with a burning fire of need. His lips trailed down her belly. His strong hands on her hips as he held her in place, exactly where he wanted her. The moment his lips kissed her lower she cried out, spreading her legs wider. Her body trembling, begging for him to claim her.

Her legs shook as he pleasured her with his mouth; she was so close to giving out under the absolute heady pleasure of bliss. She didn't want this sensation to stop, but if she didn't put a stop to it, she'd come, and she wanted to come around him.

The first time back with him, she wanted him inside her.

"Emile," she moaned. "I'm so close."

"So?" he teased.

"Oh, God."

"Tell me what you want," he murmured against her thigh.

"I want you to take me."

Emile shifted his weight, leaning over her as she wrapped her legs around him. She reached down and stroked his hard length. If he could tease her then she could torture him just a bit, too.

"Chloé, I…" He trailed off and moaned. "When you touch me like that… It's too much."

"Good."

"You're such a tease."

"As are you. I want you, Emile." She kissed him.

The head of his cock pressed against her. He thrust quickly, sinking into her, filling her completely and in exactly the way she wanted. She let out a moan of pleasure, remembering how good it felt and how long it had been.

"*Si serré*," he moaned.

"What?"

"It doesn't matter. Move with me." It wasn't a request; it was a command and she was more than happy to oblige. He moved slowly, sensuously, so she could match his rhythm, loving the feeling of them being in sync as she urged him to take her harder and faster.

A coil of heat erupted deep inside her. He reached between her legs, touching her, stroking her as she moved. She was so close. She arched her back as heady pleasure washed over her, burning through every nerve ending and fiber in her body. Her body squeezing around his thick, hard length as she tipped over the edge into joy.

Emile cried out, quickening his pace as he came, too. Holding still for a few moments before he slipped out of her, then falling beside her with a contented sigh. She rolled up next to him, tucking her head under his arm, his fingers stroking her back and her hand on his chest. She could feel his heart beating under her fingers.

This was home. It always had been.

Except, it couldn't be.

This was just a fleeting moment in time. There was an end date looming.

What did I just do?

She'd set herself up for heartbreak.

That was what she'd done.

Emile couldn't believe what had just happened and how much he'd missed being in her arms. No one had ever held a candle to Chloé and there were so many nights he thought back to their most intimate moments, missing her.

Longing for her. As much as he always tried to deny it.

She was snuggled up against him and he just breathed in the scent of her, trailing his fingers over her soft, silky skin. He was trying not to think about the fact that she would leave him again. They wanted different things. She wanted a family and he couldn't give her that. How could he keep her from fulfilling her dreams? Instead of mulling it all over or thinking about the end, he just focused on this moment with her back in his arms. Which he'd savor forever.

"What time is it?" she asked softly.

"I think midnight. Nope, I was wrong. It's one in the morning." Had he really been just holding her while she slept against him? Time was slipping by so fast.

She sat up. "Want to see if the northern lights are out?"

"I would rather stay in bed," he teased.

"I would, too, but you said you've never seen the aurora and now is your chance." She clambered out of bed and started pulling on her clothes. He watched her, enjoying his view and not wanting this night to end.

"Why don't you look and tell me? Then if it's not out there, you can come back to bed. We have an early flight tomorrow."

She rolled her eyes and smiled. "You're hopeless. Besides, you need a couple of minutes to let your eyes adjust to the darkness before they appear."

"Fine."

"For someone who said he's never seen the northern lights you're being awfully curmudgeonly about it."

He chuckled softly. "Fine, if you insist."

"I do." She grinned smugly.

He got out of bed and pulled on his clothes. "If there's no lights out there, then you owe me."

"Oh?" she teased. "And what will I owe you."

He pulled her close and kissed her playfully. "I think you know."

"I think that can be arranged. And if I'm right, then you'll owe me something for all this trouble you're putting me through."

His pulse kicked up a notch. "Oh? And what will that be?"

"We'll discuss that later." She opened the door and they stepped outside onto the small porch, shutting the door. They walked down and went around to the side of the building so they wouldn't be under the porch light. It still wasn't fully dark outside; Emile had never experienced anything like it. He'd read about it, sure, but seeing it was something so completely different.

In the sky there were a couple of stars that were bright enough to withstand the dusky midnight, but not too many.

"I see nothing," he groused.

"Look up toward the north and let your eyes adjust," she chided. "Also, stop complaining."

He smirked but did what she asked, staring at the dark sky, waiting for something. Then it was as though the sky filled with pale smoke that moved like water. The longer he stood there and stared, the more brilliant the colors became. They burst in pinks and reds, like a shimmering ribbon above them. It wasn't as bright as he'd seen in photographs, because it wasn't fully dark, but it was still mesmerizing.

"C'est incroyable!"

"It is, right?" Chloé beamed. "So beautiful."

His heart was so full and they shared a tender expression. "Not as beautiful as you are."

"Emile," she said softly and leaned her head against his shoulder while he wrapped his arm around her, just as they had earlier, but somehow so much closer after everything they'd shared. He didn't want to let her go. "What is going to happen when we head back to Montreal?" Chloé asked.

"Nothing will change. It won't be weird. I promise."

"Oh." There was hesitation in her voice. "Good."

"I care for you, Chloé. We'll be okay."

What he wanted to tell her right then was that he was still in love with her, that he never really had fallen out of love with her.

Only, he couldn't say those words. He still wasn't enough for her, and he never wanted to make her unhappy. This was all they could share together.

Nothing more.

The plane landed in Aivik Bay early the next morning. It was the same pilot. Emile had been getting updates about Immitaq Peever through the night, and she was doing well since her angioplasty. Chloé had been getting updates about Céline. She was done with her chemotherapy and the scan was showing good margins to do the surgery.

It was just a matter of when. They wanted Céline to be strong enough to withstand the long procedure, and the team had to be ready. When they got back they'd have a lot of work to do.

It felt good to focus on patients instead of talking about what had passed between them last night. It had been magical, the whole night, but both of them knew there was no future for them.

When they landed in Montreal, they parted at the hospital to clean up, before heading back later in the day. When Emile got to his father's house, his house, it just seemed even more empty than before.

It was a beautiful home and had been in the family a long time, but he couldn't help but think about that little cabin up in Aivik Bay or the crammed medical clinic where he worked in tandem with

Chloé. And then he thought of walking in Beaupré with her.

Everywhere she was, she lit up the room and he was going to miss her when she was gone.

You don't have to miss her.

He shook his head. There was no way he could ask her to stay in Montreal, not when she clearly loved her work between Ottawa and Iqaluit. And it was important work, just like his work in Montreal was. As much as he wanted her to stay, to have a surgeon of her caliber on his team, he couldn't ask that of her.

She deserved her happiness.

She deserved her life, not to be chained to the same place he was. She deserved a family.

It wasn't her duty to stay here, but it was his.

CHAPTER ELEVEN

A week later

ONCE THEY GOT back to the hospital Emile went to check on the Peevers, and Chloé went to see Céline. It was then she had to throw herself into the planning of the surgery. It was hard to believe that a month had passed since she'd come to Montreal and reconnected with Emile, but only a week since they'd deeply connected again.

At least, that was how she saw it.

True to Emile's word, nothing had gone weird between them, and she was very thankful for that. They were professional and friendly. It was like their night of passion never happened

That was what they'd agreed, but in truth, she now missed him more than ever.

She missed being in his arms, kissing him, waking up next to him. The bed at her hotel was lonely.

And she wanted more of him.

Which was exactly what she'd been afraid would happen.

I could transfer to Montreal?

Maybe she could still do her rotations in Iqaluit from Montreal? Maybe the board of directors at Hôpital de Ville-Marie would allow that? But it would be tricky. Ottawa and Iqaluit worked together and right now, she had an awful lot of funding helping her work between the two hospitals.

There was nothing really tying her to Ottawa, just the proximity to Iqaluit and the rapport. The real problem was Emile's steadfast determination on the topic of kids. He had made it very clear that he didn't want a family or a relationship because work came first. She also knew how scared he was of it, because of what happened between his parents. Chloé understood it; she didn't have to like it, but she understood it all the same.

Was family something she was willing to give up? Chloé wasn't sure. If she really wanted marriage and children, despite all her fears about illness and juggling work, she would've found someone else, but she hadn't.

She just didn't know, and it was all so confusing. Her brain was working so hard to try to figure out a way to make it work so that she could stay with Emile. But would he even *want* her to stay? When they'd gotten together that night it was on the promise that it would just be for one night, and with the assumption when the time came she'd leave for good. And he certainly hadn't hinted that she should stay and work at the hospital…

Nuka, you can follow your heart.

Chloé let out an exasperated sigh in frustration. She hated all this wishy-washy nonsense. All this thinking and worrying over something she walked away from years ago.

Except she wasn't sure that she ever actually did walk away.

As she sat there at her computer mulling all this over, she got a ping that the latest imaging and lab work for Céline had come in. She quickly chased those thoughts away and pulled up the information.

Céline's blood work looked good. She was stronger than she had been last week. Her prealbumin was high and white cell count was manageable and the tumor hadn't grown again in the past seven days, which meant the surgical margins were good. Now was the perfect moment.

It was time to do the surgery.

She sent the files to the team who would be joining her on the surgery and then got up to make her way over to Emile's office. Usually, he'd be walking the floors and working with patients, but she knew he had several meetings today so maybe he'd be easy to find.

As she walked through the hallway, she passed the paintings of his ancestors. All the Moreaus that had worked and bled for this hospital before Emile. Their sour expressions. Once she'd thought they were just stoic, but now she got the feeling they were dour, looking down at her. She felt bad that Emile had to deal with this indignation every day.

This judgment.

Why did a bunch of dead ancestors hold such sway over him?

And looking at Emile's father's portrait, she

couldn't help but wonder what the senior Dr. Moreau had really felt.

Did he have any regrets about pressuring his son, for breaking Marguerite's heart? And why did Emile want to make *this* man so proud?

She shuddered and quickly made her way over to Emile's office.

Donna was working on her computer as she approached. "Doctor MacDonald, he asked me to send you in once you arrived."

"How did he know I was coming?" she asked, puzzled.

Donna smiled. "He received the files on Céline and he's expecting you."

Chloé laughed. "I don't suppose you can book me an operating room time for tomorrow?"

"Already done. I emailed you and the rest of the team."

"Perfect, Donna. You're a gem." Chloé knocked and then stepped inside Emile's office. "Hey, you all ready?"

"Glad you're here. I had Donna book the operating room," Emile said, looking up from behind his desk. Behind him were windows that overlooked Montreal. It was a stunning view and she was a bit taken aback as she realized that in her month here she hadn't actually been in his office. Emile had come to hers, or she had spoken with him in the hall.

He looked over his shoulder. "What?"

"I just realized I haven't been in your office before. Jeez, I have a little hovel in the corner and you have a penthouse."

Emile shrugged. "It is a nice view, but I barely spend time here. So, are you ready to do this surgery?"

Chloé nodded. "Have you called Céline's parents? I would like to go over the procedure with them this afternoon."

"I have," he stated. "Only because I was talking to Agathe about Céline when the information came in. Parliament is on a summer break, so she is here already. If you want to go down and talk to them, there's no time like the present."

"Good, because Céline will be in the hospital for a bit longer. I want to make sure she gets one more round of chemo after she heals from surgery. Just so we can make sure we kill off all the cancer cells." Chloé hesitated for a moment, wondering if he'd ask her to stay and see that through.

But Emile didn't respond. It cut her to the quick.

She cleared her throat. "I will leave post-operative instructions for her care, as I'm just here for the surgery."

A strange look passed across his face, almost like he was surprised, and she wondered if he had been expecting her to stay, after all. "I appreciate that."

Ask me to stay. I'll consider staying if you ask me to stay. She kept those thoughts to herself.

Instead, she asked, "Are you ready for this surgery?"

"I am. It will be long, but I'm glad it will be done for Céline. It's her best possible chance."

Chloé nodded. "It is."

"Well, let's go down and speak to Agathe and Tomas." He stood up and grabbed his white lab coat.

Suddenly, things were awkward again and she didn't know why. Maybe it was all in her head, because her own stupid heart was involved now. And she was realizing that even despite her best efforts, she loved him and wanted to stay here with him. After this surgery was done, it was going to be so hard to get into her car and drive back to Ottawa.

They made their way down to the pediatric ward and sure enough, Céline's parents were in her room. Agathe was pacing. Just from watching them through the window, Chloé could see the look of worry etched into their faces. The same expression that her parents had worn so often when Immi was sick in the hospital or faced yet another surgery.

It wasn't new on Agathe's and Tomas's faces, but today it was hitting harder. Perhaps because Emile knew about Immi, and Chloé didn't have to paper her own pain and trepidation over with laughter and happiness.

She was feeling a lot of emotions today. Even though the margins looked good, the tumor had shrunk and Céline was strong, there was always the unknown. The small percent of uncertainty she couldn't control.

"Hey," Emile said softly. "This will be okay."

"Of course," she agreed quickly. "Why wouldn't it be?"

"You're thinking of your sister again, aren't you?"

She smiled slightly. "I am. I'm glad I don't have to try and hide it from you."

I can be myself around you. I don't have to make you happy. But she didn't say that out loud, either. How could she be a burden to him? He had a lot to shoulder here, too. Sure, he'd seen that side of her, the grief, but how long could he really tolerate it?

All he knew before was her sunshine. That was what people were drawn to. Maybe if he'd seen the real her all this time, he'd have grown quickly tired of her.

Emile smiled at her, encouraging her. "Let's go give Agathe and Tomas the good news."

"Yes. Let's do this." She took a deep breath, steeled her resolve and locked away everything she was feeling, to plaster that bright sunshine smile on her face. Céline's parents needed that brave face from her. They needed her confidence.

As they walked in, Agathe stopped pacing and sat down next to her husband, clutching his hand. Céline was sleeping in her bed, still holding a tablet where she'd been playing some kind of game. Chloé could still hear the music from it. It was precious.

"Well?" Agathe asked. "She had scans early this morning and blood work."

"She did. She's ready for her surgery," Chloé stated. "I'm going to start her on preoperative antibiotics and no food or drink after midnight."

"It's tomorrow?" Tomas asked.

"*Oui*," Emile answered. "We want to make sure we get a head start and not give the tumor time to grow. It was aggressive when you brought Céline to us, so we don't want to give it any more chances."

"That's understandable," Tomas stated, and he squeezed his wife's hand.

"What time tomorrow?" Agathe asked, her voice shaking.

"Seven in the morning," Chloé responded. "It will be a long procedure. It's open-heart surgery and then Céline will be in the intensive care unit for a couple of days, sedated and intubated to allow her to heal. It will be a hard procedure."

A tear slipped from Agathe's eyes. "I understand. It's the only way, right? We can't shrink it any further."

"You're correct," Emile responded. "The chemotherapy did work on shrinking the tumor, but it will grow back and spread. Once it spreads to other parts of her body, there's not much hope."

"This is our time to take care of it," Chloé reiterated. "It's hard, but she's young and kids bounce back incredibly fast."

Tomas nodded. "Okay. How long will the procedure take?"

"About six hours," Chloé stated.

"That's a long time," Agathe murmured.

"It is, but it's complex. After her surgery and after she heals, we'll put her on one last round of chemotherapy to really make sure we've killed off as much of the cancer cells as we can. Once that's complete, she'll be able to ring the bell and go home," Chloé said, smiling as brightly as she could muster.

"Home?" Agathe looked down at her daughter and smiled tenderly. "That's always been my hope. Thank you, Doctors."

"Don't thank us yet. I'll send down a resident to go over the paperwork and talk about the risks with you," Emile said. "But I'm pretty confident that those won't be an issue."

"If you need anything else, please let us know," Chloé added. "We'll see you both tomorrow morning."

Chloé and Emile left. She glanced back to see Agathe and Tomas hug. A sob welled up in her throat watching them. They had each other to lean on. Just like her parents had. Despite everything, Céline was a lucky girl.

"Well, now we should go over the procedure with the team and then you and I both need to get some good sleep tonight," Emile remarked.

"Agreed. It's going to be an early day tomorrow." She worried her bottom lip. "I can't believe my time here is almost done."

"Me either, but you'll be glad to get back to your own hospital and your apartment, *non*?"

Well, that is a finality.

"Sure," she said, hoping her voice didn't break. "Well, let's go assemble the team and go over the plan of attack."

He nodded. "*Bonne.*"

Chloé couldn't let herself think about her own feelings or her heart or anything like that right now. Céline was counting on her. She wasn't going to let that little girl not have a chance at life. She'd been brought here to Montreal for this.

This was what she did best.

This was her life. And it would have to be enough.

Nuka, I'm right here with you. I always am.

Chloé took a deep breath and closed her eyes to calm herself. Hearing Immi's voice in her head was a good thing. She always took it as a good sign. So she focused on that.

Céline was prepped and ready to go. The surgery had started.

Emile had made the first cuts and Chloé was waiting to do the delicate work on the heart, which couldn't happen until Céline was on the bypass machine.

Chloé had actually slept that night. Maybe it was because she had *finally* allowed herself to come to the full realization that this was all she'd ever have with Emile. That it was okay to move on.

Even though part of her really didn't want to.

Focus.

This was her big moment. So many surgeons would be watching and learning from her. She opened her eyes and looked up at the gallery. It was packed with residents and interns who weren't part of this surgery.

She wasn't used to working in a jam-packed operating room. A gallery was fine, but she didn't want to have extra bodies in the operating room with her. This was a delicate procedure. She tore her gaze away from the crowds and instead focused on Emile's work. It was always calming watching a skilled surgeon at work, and Emile was no exception.

She stood there, patiently waiting. Ready to go.

"Okay, put her on bypass and start the clock," Emile stated. Their gazes locked as he stepped back. "She's ready for you, Doctor MacDonald."

Chloé nodded and stepped up to the table. "Scalpel."

The scrub nurse placed what she needed in her palm. They had practiced the steps, the instruments were ready and now it was time for her to take this tiny nonbeating broken heart and repair it. Remove the cancer that grew in there and give the little girl a chance at life.

Right here with you, Nuka. You've got this.

Chloé didn't even think about the clock that was counting the time. There was only so long Céline could be on the bypass machine. Only so long it would be safe.

Emile was close to her. Watching her.

"I'm right here," he whispered in her ear. "You're doing beautifully."

"I hope I'm giving enough instruction for everyone," she said out loud. "Sometimes I think in my head, but I don't know that I'm actually talking out loud."

"Yes, Doctor MacDonald. You are," Emile reassured. "All you're missing is a bad pun or a dad joke."

She smiled to herself and continued the work.

She knew the steps like clockwork in her head and she wanted to make sure she was imparting her wisdom on everyone here.

She made a cut and exposed the tumor. "See how the tumor has shrunk? It will be easier to get better margins now and allow the muscle to repair."

Chloé carefully excised the tumor from the heart muscle, making sure she got it all and placed it into a bag for pathology.

Once she was sure all the cancerous material was removed, she began to repair the muscle and put the heart back together.

If only someone could put *hers* back together.

"Clamps, please," she asked.

Emile reached down beside her and clamped an artery so she could stitch it back up. As she continued to drone on about the repair, she felt lighter, because the surgery was going well. Once she went over her work with Emile, she laid down her instruments.

"Everything looks good. Let's bring her off bypass and check the flow for leaks," she asked.

"Yes, Doctor MacDonald," Dr. LaCroix stated. The machines flicked off; the clamps were removed.

Please. Chloé said a silent prayer, the way she always did when she'd completed heart surgery and they were checking for leaks.

The heart pinked back up and there was a beat. A steady beat with no leaking, no bubbling, just a heart.

There was clapping and Chloé smiled under her surgical mask, breathing a sigh of relief.

"She's all yours to close up, Doctor Moreau," Chloé stated, stepping back from the table.

"Excellent job, Doctor MacDonald," Emile said and he got to work closing up Céline. Chloé checked the clock and was relieved to see that it hadn't taken the full six hours to remove the tumor.

You never knew until you opened the patient up. She had explained that to Agathe and Tomas, but she was glad Céline's tumor had shrunk so much and Céline didn't have to be on bypass for any longer.

She took another shaky breath. She felt like crying.

Tears of relief, but also of mourning that her time here was over.

Emile and his staff could handle her post-operative care. There was no need for her to stay.

Unless Emile asked.

Nuka, would you stay, though?

Could she give up the thought of kids for a chance with Emile? Her career for him?

She still wasn't sure. She was in love with Emile. She just wasn't sure if that was enough, because to be with him meant sacrificing so much.

Even if he did ask her to stay, there was always a chance that they would just drift apart. Hospital came first for him, and her work was important, too. She couldn't ask him to give up a piece of himself for her.

That was not how love worked. Love meant supporting your partner, not giving up on yourself.

Emile didn't usually follow his patients from the PACU to the intensive care unit, but this time he had to. He was still in awe from the surgery and the fact that little Céline, with such a big tumor, was still alive.

He was also in awe of Chloé's skill. The surgery and her teaching had been recorded with Agathe's and Tomas's permission; they wanted others to learn. And Chloé removed the tumor with such care and talent.

She had left once he'd finished closing, but as he followed the gurney to the intensive care unit, he found her waiting there.

"Vitals good?" she asked as Céline was wheeled into the ICU pod.

"Stable," he replied.

Chloé smiled; he could see the exhaustion in her face. "That's great news."

"Shall we go tell Céline's parents?"

"You haven't spoken to them yet?" she wondered out loud.

"No. We both should do that. Besides, it's the best part of the job."

Chloé nodded, beaming. "Yes. Let's do that."

They walked in silence to the waiting room. It

was hitting him that soon Chloé would leave and there was nothing he could do to entice her to stay. The board would do anything they could to keep her here in Montreal, but he knew how much the north meant to her.

After going to Aivik Bay with her, he understood why she did what she did.

Just like she understood why he did what he did. The legacy of his family here in Montreal and the benefits of this hospital.

They were on different paths, the ones that they'd always been on.

It was breaking his heart, because he did love her, but his commitment was to this hospital. He wouldn't get involved with her and ruin what they had, just like his father had ruined his own marriage. He wouldn't hurt her like that. He couldn't do that to her.

If he was in a different place and didn't have this burden of a family name looming over him, if he knew how to be a good father and husband, then he could give her more. He could have that life with her.

He just didn't know how.

So as much as he wanted to ask her to stay, he just couldn't.

Céline's parents were in a separate waiting room, because the last thing Agathe needed was people bugging her about the government. Agathe and Tomas stood when they entered, and Emile could see the dark circles under their eyes.

"She made it through and is in the ICU," he stated.

Agathe gasped, covering her mouth as Tomas wrapped his arm around her.

"I removed all the tumor. Pathology is checking the mass. I think she'll require one more round of chemotherapy to make sure all the cancer cells are gone. First, she'll be intubated and in the ICU for a couple of days," Chloé explained. "It all looks really promising, though."

"I can't thank you both enough. When can we see her?" Agathe asked.

"I'll take you now," Emile offered.

Agathe and Tomas both thanked Chloé and left with him. At the door, Emile looked back at Chloé and sent her a congratulatory smile, trying to boost her up as he walked away. He wanted to see her off, but first he had a duty to his patients like he always did.

When Agathe and Tomas were settled in the ICU he did a quick check on Céline, then, happy with her progress, he made his way up to Chloé's office, knowing that was where she'd be.

When he got to her office, her door was open and she was packing up her computer.

"You're heading out?" he asked, trying to swallow the emotions that were crying out in him, telling him to beg her to stay. Not to leave. To give her everything she wanted, only he couldn't. He was fighting inside.

There was no way he would hurt her like his father did to his mother. It would be too cruel; to know he'd crushed her beautiful soul by not giving her what she needed—by stopping her seeking it with somebody else, because he selfishly wanted her.

And Emile wasn't cruel. He wasn't coldhearted.

He had to let her go.

He'd rather do that now than have her hate him down the road.

"Tomorrow. One more night in the hotel." She smiled, but the smile didn't reach her eyes.

"Your hospital will be happy to have you back."

"Indeed. Thank you again for allowing me to see a couple of patients here in Montreal. I appreciate that."

He nodded. "Of course. The board…"

"Yes?" she asked.

"The board and Céline's parents were thankful for all you did."

She nodded her head. "It was my pleasure."

Stay. For me.

Only he couldn't get those words out. He couldn't say them. He wasn't going to trap her here with him. She could be free; he couldn't. How could he break her heart?

He didn't even know how she felt. Neither of them had expressed love, not here in the present. He wasn't even sure he knew how to show it. His father never had. All he had taught Emile was devotion to work. And he had once promised his mother love, but it had just turned to sadness and bitterness.

The idea that Emile might do that to Chloé tore at the very fibers of his soul. He just couldn't risk it.

"I hope…" he managed. "I hope we can work together in the future again sometime."

Their gazes met, her eyes sad. "That's it?"

"Is there supposed to be something more?"

A strange expression crossed her face. "No. I guess not."

"You belong in the north and I belong here."

"Why?" she asked. The smile was gone. Her lips set in a thin, firm line. No twinkle in her eyes. Already, he could see he was diminishing her light and he hated himself for that.

"My family."

"What family?" she asked sadly. "All I see are people who caused you misery hanging from the walls."

Emile frowned. "That may be so, but I am not the only one clinging to a past, to a duty."

Her eyes widened in shock, before they narrowed. "You're right. My work in the north is because my sister died due to lack of care. Every life I save is another Immitaq. Your father is dead. You can't earn his love and respect now," she said firmly, with a hint of bitterness.

He didn't want them to part ways again in an argument. He regretted that the last time when they'd broken up. He wasn't going to let it be like that again.

"I can't give you what you want, Chloé."

"And what's that?"

"A life. Family. My work comes first and you know this."

"I suppose I do. I'm glad you know what you want." There was a hint of bitterness there, too. It tore at his heart, but this was better.

You mean easier.

He shook that thought away. "It was a pleasure working with you again, Doctor MacDonald." He turned and left her.

It was the hardest thing he'd ever done, walking away from her again. With each step, his heart tore open.

He hated himself for hurting her again.

This was why he hadn't wanted to get involved with her. It was why he wanted to keep his distance.

The problem was he could never resist her. How could he resist someone he loved so much?

CHAPTER TWELVE

One week later

CHLOÉ HAD BEEN gone a week. And like a fool, Emile walked by her office every day.

He was barely sleeping, because he couldn't stop thinking about her. He missed her, but he'd pushed her away for her own good. There was no way he was going to take a chance on love and ruin it like his father did. He'd seen firsthand how it nearly destroyed his mother. There was no way that he could do that to Chloé.

She was too nice, too happy. She was all things good and bright. How could he dim that light?

In spite of all the hardships that she'd endured and the pain of losing her twin, she saw the brighter side of life.

He was too afraid of turning into his father.

Haven't you already?

Céline was doing well and responding favorably to the chemotherapy, but seeing her or Immitaq Peever reminded him of Chloé. She was now everywhere in the halls of the Hôpital de Ville-Marie. Every day he still walked past the dour faces of his relatives, but now looking at them just made him so angry.

Angry that they had trapped him here.

Trapped him in this legacy that he wasn't sure that he wanted anymore.

All his life he'd been told he wanted this to the point that he believed it. Now he wasn't too sure.

What am I doing?

Every day since Chloé had left, he'd grown more frustrated and angry at himself.

Finally, he decided to go against the grain and take a day off. He packed a small bag, got into his car and headed to Beaupré, to the only person who would understand what he was grappling with.

His maman.

Driving to his mother's home, he recalled the laughter the last time they drove there. Chloé's sense of wonder over the falls. The moments they'd shared in Quebec City. Just every joke, every conversation. How much she'd loved every little bit of his home, making him see it through new eyes.

Now this drive didn't seem so magical. Instead, it hurt.

When he pulled up to his mother's house, Marguerite was outside, puttering around in her front garden. She seemed surprised when he parked the car and got out.

"Emile?" she asked, stunned. "It's the middle of the week."

"Can't I visit you during the week?" he asked, amused.

"You don't usually. You're always busy with work." She pulled off her gardening gloves. "Are you okay? Where is *ma chouette*?"

"Chloé returned back to Ottawa. Her rotation in Iqaluit was starting and she had to go back." What he didn't tell his mother was that he'd pushed her away.

Her mother looked crestfallen. "I'm happy she's doing her work, but I'm sad her visit here was so short. I adore her."

"I noticed, given what you call her." Emile locked his car and headed over to his mother, kissing her on the head. "How are you feeling? I hope you're still taking breaks?"

"I'm not an invalid, Emile. And yes, I do take rests. Would you like to sit down?"

Emile nodded and took a seat on one of the white rattan chairs on her front porch. He could hear the river babbling across the road, the birds trilling in the air. So different from the city. He'd forgotten how much he loved it out here, the summers he spent here with his mother.

It was nice to take a moment and breathe. He realized he hadn't done that in a long time.

"So, why have you come?" his mother asked.

"Do you not want me here?"

"Oh no, I do. I'm glad."

"I needed… I needed to breathe." What he needed was Chloé and a life with her; he needed the sunshine back in his life, but he didn't know how to say it. He didn't even dare to dream it.

"You love her. Don't you?" his mother asked, taking the seat next to him.

"What?" he asked, stunned.

His mother looked at him with reproach. "I know you, Emile. You love her. You always have."

"And if I did? She works too far away. She won't come to Montreal."

"Did you ask her?" his mother asked.

"No. How can I ask her when her life is up north? She's doing something good there."

"I agree," his mother stated. "You can go on rotation there, too, you know."

"I can't do that. I'm head of cardiothoracic surgery. I have a legacy to uphold."

"Whose?"

He sighed and scrubbed a hand over his face. "Father's."

His mother shook her head. "You don't have to live up to him. Why are you trying to earn his love? He loved you, Emile."

"He didn't love me, Maman. How could you say that?"

"He loved both of us." His mother's voice shook.

"If he loved both of us, then why did you leave?"

Marguerite sighed. "I left because yes, he loved his work more. Because he was living up to his father's expectations. Always chasing that love. Just like you, and I hate seeing you doing the same."

It felt like everything Emile thought he knew came crashing down. That was not what he expected to learn about his father. It wasn't the man he thought he remembered… But it sounded exactly like the man he'd become, too.

They weren't totally the same. He valued his connection with his patients; he was opening up more. He had pushed Chloé away for her own good so he wouldn't hurt her like his father had done to his mother.

I still put the hospital first.

In that way they were the same. But what if it didn't have to be like that? What if Emile could have more?

"How can I walk away from the hospital?" His voice shook as all the probabilities played around in his head.

"You don't have to. You just have to walk away from the head of cardiothoracic to take up work in Iqaluit. Can you do that?'

It was a fair question.

Could he? It wasn't like he was leaving Montreal or his family behind here, and he would be working toward something he'd always wanted. Freedom, love and doing what he was passionate about.

Being up in Aivik Bay had been amazing. It had given him that thrill like the one he'd felt when he first started medicine.

Maybe he did deserve more than somebody else's dream. He deserved happiness, and going after it didn't make him less of a surgeon.

"Well?" his mother asked. "I'm sure the hospital will let you do rotation up north."

"I can, but that's not all."

"What, then?"

"Chloé wants a family, marriage, children. How can I give her those things? Look how..." It was hard to finish the sentence. It was hard to speak because it seemed so obvious, suddenly, that it wasn't enough justification to push Chloé away.

He loved her. Could he rise above his father? The idea terrified him, but he wanted that life of love and joy with Chloé.

"How you were raised?" Marguerite asked quietly.

"*Oui.*" His voice shook.

"It's my greatest regret I didn't fight harder for you. Your father had more money and sway, but you can break the pattern, Emile. I know I say you're like your father, but there's me in there, too. If you were truly like him we wouldn't be having this conversation."

She was right. If he was truly like his father he wouldn't be here. He wouldn't miss Chloé so much.

"Do you still love him?"

"I did, but it was better we were apart. We were so very different. I don't regret it, though. I had you."

It warmed his heart to hear her say that.

"Chloé and I are different, too."

"Not that much."

Emile nodded, swallowing a hard lump in his throat. "I want to be happy, Maman."

She smiled and placed her hand on his knee. "You deserve to be happy, Emile. Go and find your happiness. You deserve love and you won't get it from someone who is no longer here, but I want you to know that he did love you. He loved you very much, even if he couldn't show it. I do, too, even though I wasn't there."

And that was the crux of the matter. He *could* love Chloé. He knew that in his heart, but he needed to show up for her. He needed to demonstrate he would be her partner. That he was there.

Was he scared? Yes, because he might've already blown it, but he had to take that risk and show her he was here for her.

He loved her.

And he wasn't going to leave.

Emile leaned over and kissed his mother on her head. "Thank you."

"If you're looking for my blessing regarding *ma chouette*, you have it. Just in case that wasn't clear." His mother winked.

"No, not clear at all," Emile teased.

Marguerite smiled. "Now, I believe you have decisions to make and probably travel arrangements? If you have the wedding in Iqaluit, I am quite willing and able to fly up there."

"Good to know, Maman." He got up and headed to his car.

"One more thing," his mother called out.

"What's that?"

"Give her my love. I can't wait to see her again."

"She might turn me down."

"She won't."

Emile nodded. "I'll tell her. I'll call you later, Maman."

It was scary, giving up the legacy that had been

instilled in him his whole life, but when the decision had been made it felt as though a huge weight had been lifted off his shoulders. And for the first time in a long time Emile finally felt free.

His only hope now was that he wasn't too late.

That he hadn't hurt Chloé too much, and that he still had a chance with her. Even if it took him some time to convince her, when he got to Iqaluit and declared himself, he wasn't going to let her go for a third time.

This time, he was playing for keeps.

He was playing forever.

One week later

"You have been kind of down since you came up here. Thought summer was your favorite time to come here?"

Chloé looked up at her *anaana* and realized she had been just sitting there, staring out through the front window of her parents' home, holding her cup of coffee, not drinking. It was cold now and a bit congealed because her mom had made her father's special camp coffee.

"How long have I been sitting here?" Chloé asked.

"Since I poured you that coffee," *Anaana* remarked, giving her a knowing glance.

"The coffee may have turned into some form of blob-like life," Chloé joked halfheartedly.

Her mother snorted. "I wouldn't be surprised. What's eating you?"

"Sorry, just lost in thoughts."

"You've been lost in thoughts since you got off the plane a week ago," *Anaana* stated. "What's going on with you? Usually, you come here for your rotation and you're so bouncy and happy…"

"I don't have to always be happy, *Anaana*," Chloé snapped. She sat down her coffee mug and rubbed her temples.

"Hey," *Anaana* said, sitting across from her. "What's going on with you? You don't usually get snippy."

"I'm sorry. Just…tired. A couple of weeks ago I was in Montreal and doing a complicated surgery on a child and…just tired."

It was a lie, but she didn't have the energy or the need to burden her mother. She didn't want to be a hardship to her parents. Ever. And swallowing her emotions was habit.

Nuka, you can talk to Anaana.

"Chloé, somehow I don't believe you," her mother said gently. "Tell me."

"No. I don't want to…"

"Don't want to what?" *Anaana* asked.

"Upset you." Her lips trembled. "I'm happy and bubbly because… I didn't want to worry you ever."

"What're you talking about?"

"*Anaana*, when Immitaq…" She swallowed the lump forming in her throat, trying to hold it back. All those years of grief that she had to keep bottled up. All the times she didn't talk about Immi to her parents because she didn't want them to be sad, it was all about to erupt out of her again.

This time she wasn't sure that she could hold anything back. She'd been bottling her grief for so long and her bottle was filled. It was overwhelming how completely the emotion consumed her.

Nuka, tell Anaana.

"When Immi died, I made a promise to myself to never cause you or *Ataata* any kind of pain or grief. I wanted you both to know that I was okay."

"Oh, Chloé," her mother said softly. "You didn't need to do that. You were a kid and..."

"*Anaana*, no, it was okay." She brushed away tears.

"No, it wasn't. I was the parent. You weren't and that wasn't your responsibility. So I'm sorry that you felt it was."

Chloé began to cry then. Full-on ugly cry. "Everything I do, my work, it's so others don't have to go through what you and *Ataata* had to. I'm saving others."

"I know," her mother's voice broke. "And I'm so very proud of you. But this isn't your burden to bear."

"How could it not be?"

"What do you mean?"

"I survived."

Her mother's lips trembled and she held Chloé's face, bringing her forehead to hers. "And I'm thankful every day you did. The way you use your life to heal makes me so proud. I want you to live the way *you* want, though."

Chloé closed her eyes. Hot tears rushing down her cheeks. "I'm trying."

Her mother let her sit back. "I think that something else is bothering you. It's not just Immi. So tell me. I'm here for you. I'm your parent, tell me."

Chloé sighed. "It's Emile. I saw him again and… I'm still in love with him."

"And that's a problem?"

"He is so tied to Montreal and the hospital where his family has worked that… I think he's afraid of love. Afraid of hurting me."

"That sounds slightly familiar."

Chloé looked at her mother. "What do you mean?"

"You were so scared of hurting us you've been bottling up your emotions for so long. Afraid of having any kind of happiness, because you've dedicated your life to saving Immitaq."

"Yes," Chloé whispered.

"Immitaq is gone," her mother said. "You are still here and you deserve happiness."

"I know," Chloé said. "The problem is…" Now she was talking she couldn't hold any of it in. "He didn't want me. He said he can't give me what I need."

"Are you sure about that?" her mother asked.

"He didn't ask me to stay." Chloé felt the tears slip down her cheeks and she brushed them away. "I love him, *Anaana*."

Her mother got up and held her and she clung to

her. "I know you do, and you should fight for what you want. You deserve it. And you don't need to hide your emotions away anymore, Chloé. Not from me. Promise?"

Chloé nodded. "I promise, *Anaana*. I don't know what the next steps are, though."

"I can't tell you that, but I can tell you, you'll be late for your clinic if you sit around here any longer."

Chloé chuckled through the last of her tears. "Okay. I better clean up. I'll see you later tonight?"

Anaana nodded. "Take *Ataata*'s ATV. He won't miss it."

"I thought he wanted to take a load to the dump?" Chloé asked.

"He'll survive. He just goes out there to hang out with Jerry Aglook."

"Remind me later to talk to Jerry about his French words. He gave me bad advice in school." Chloé was feeling much better as she washed her face.

"And that surprises you?" *Anaana* asked, making her smile.

She grabbed her jacket and her briefcase and headed outside. Her *ataata*'s ATV was ready and waiting. She took his helmet and climbed on it, starting the engine and driving toward the hospital.

She waved at a few people she knew then parked the ATV in the parking lot, leaving the helmet on the seat, knowing it would be safe.

She really didn't know what the next steps would be, but she knew she was going to tell Emile how she felt and go from there. If he still didn't want her, she could move on and heal. Right now, she had to focus on her clinic work.

She headed inside, trying to get to her office when she saw the chief of the hospital approaching her.

"Ah, Doctor MacDonald, I have great news. There's a new doctor here scoping out our hospital. Wants to be part of the cardiac rotation program and we really want to have him."

"Great," Chloé said brightly.

"Would you show him around? He says he knows you."

Her heart skipped a beat. "What?"

"From Montreal. A Doctor Moreau," the chief stated.

"That's impossible. The Doctor Moreau I know is the head of cardiothoracic surgery at Hôpital de Ville-Marie. There's no way a head surgeon could be part of this rotation."

"He was head, but now he's just a surgeon there," the chief stated. "The new head sent him a recommendation. So can you show him around? Convince him to join?"

"Sure," Chloé said, stunned, and took his file. She headed into her office, her pulse thundering between her ears as she opened the door. Emile was sitting there waiting for her. His eyes lit up when he saw her.

"Emile?" she asked, surprised. "What're you… Why? I have so many questions."

Emile grinned. "I'm sure you do. *Oui*, I'm here about joining the rotation program, though I have some stipulations about that, and I am no longer head of cardiothoracic at Hôpital de Ville-Marie. I stepped down and became an attending. So I have more flexibility."

"Why?" Chloé asked, shutting the door behind her.

"Because I can't do this program being the head."

"I understand, but…what are you doing here?" Maybe she should've drunk that coffee.

There was a nervous energy emanating from him, something so unlike him. She felt like she should sit down, only she couldn't, too nervous herself.

Emile ran his hand through his hair, making it stand on end. Then his gaze locked on to her and his eyes twinkled. He smiled at her tenderly, just like he used to do. "I'm in love with you, Chloé. I've always been in love with you."

Chloé's pulse was pounding between her ears and her heart felt like it was going to bust out of her chest. She couldn't quite believe what she was hearing. It had been what she'd longed for for years, since she left Emile. It was the stuff of fairy tales, a dream. She gripped the doorknob behind her and blinked a few times before she was finally able to speak. "I love you, too. I always have."

Her pulse began to race and all she wanted was to be in his arms, but she still wasn't sure if she trusted him. If this wasn't all a delusional hallucination.

Emile took a step closer to her. "I want to work up here with you. Together."

"We only allow those accommodations for married couples," Chloé stated, trying to still figure out how to read him.

"*Oui.* I understand. Which is why I want to marry you."

She found it hard to breathe, the gasp of surprise catching in her throat. "You…what?"

He chuckled softly. "I said I want to marry you."

She shook her head in disbelief. It was all just too good to be true. "Is that so? What about kids and family?"

"I want that."

"You didn't before." It came out as a whisper. If only it were true.

"I was wrong, but I only want that with you. I can give you that. Let me come up here and show you."

"But I mean…you love Montreal. It was evident. Are you sure you can walk away from that for months at a time?"

She worried her bottom lip. As much as she wanted this, she didn't want him to give up everything, either. He should be happy, too.

Then Emile smiled at her tenderly and she believed him. All the worry melted away as he brushed his knuckles over her cheek. The old Emile was there, in those blue eyes, and she melted from his touch.

"*Oui.* I can. The thing is, I do love Quebec. It's been my life's work. But I think seeing it from your perspective when you were in Montreal was a way for me to let it go, because the truth of the matter is, I love you more. Much more than a legacy or a hospital or a city. I was spending my life chasing my father's love and approval. You were right—the problem with that is he's gone. You're here and I can't seem to let you go. I'm terrified of hurting you or turning into my father, but I think you won't let that happen."

Tears stung her eyes and she cleared her throat, her smile a bit wobbly. "You're right. I won't. And… I can transfer from Ottawa to Montreal. If your new head will have me."

"She will." Emile grinned, so cocky and sure of himself. It made her laugh. Her Emile was back, truly back. He tipped her chin and kissed her gently, making her melt. "So? Does that mean you'll marry me?"

"Since you're stooping to blackmail…"

Emile blinked. "What?"

Chloé grinned, enjoying the torture. "You'll only come here to work if it's with me so I *have* to marry you."

He groaned. "Are you serious?"

Chloé laughed, then sobered up. She thought of her conversation with *Anaana* about hiding her feelings. She didn't have to do that with him. She knew that now. "I will be serious sometimes. But I think I can be with you. You're the first person I shared Immitaq with. You're the first person since her that's made me feel safe."

"I'm glad to hear that."

Chloé kissed him again. "I may not always be bright and sunshiny, though."

"It's okay. I just want to be with you. So, do I have the job?"

She grinned. "Perhaps. I do have to interview you first."

He cocked an eyebrow. "*Chloé...*"

"*Oui*," she whispered.

"And, what about the other question I asked?"

She wrapped her arms around his neck and made a face like she was thinking hard about it. "*Oui.*"

He kissed her again, deeply, making her weak in the knees. She was bursting with a happiness she couldn't comprehend. It wasn't a facade she put on to make others happy—she was truly reveling in the fairy-tale moment that she never thought she would ever have. Her happily-ever-after.

"I love you, Chloé," he whispered huskily against her ear.

"I love you, too, Emile. But I also have a *stipulation* before we announce our engagement to the whole world."

"And what's that?"

"You have to take the ATV in the parking lot and drive over to my parents' house and ask my *ataata* permission to marry me."

Emile's eyes widened in horror. "I don't even know where your parents' house is?"

"Just ask people as you drive toward the docks, then they can tell you."

He frowned. "You're not going to make this easy for me, are you?"

"You want to work in the north, this is an initiation like no other." She kissed him again. "Do I have to ask permission from your mother?"

"No, she adores you. She wants her *chouette* to visit her again, and she wants the wedding to be up here."

Chloé laughed. "I think we can make that happen."

For the first time since Immi died, she felt free. Like she didn't have to pretend anymore. She hadn't been sure if she deserved a happy-ever-after, but now she knew that she did.

And she was getting the one she'd always dreamed of.

An equal one.

EPILOGUE

One year later

EMILE PULLED UP to the familiar white house in Beaupré. His mother was outside waiting, sitting on the porch, like she usually did in the summer.

"I wonder if she's been waiting out there since we told her we landed in Montreal yesterday?" Chloé asked, a hint of humor in her voice.

"Of course. Are you surprised by this?" Emile asked, looking through the rearview mirror at his wife sitting in the back next to the car seat.

"No. Not at all," Chloé responded.

"She is not going to sit inside patiently and wait for the arrival of her granddaughter." Emile climbed out of the car and then opened the back door to take out the car seat, which had the most precious bundle in the world inside it.

His daughter.

Chloé got out of the car.

"I'm so glad you're all here," his mother said loudly, rushing down her path, her arms wide-open. "*Ma chouette!* You look wonderful."

"Marguerite, it's so good to see you again."

Emile watched as his mother embraced Chloé, kissing her on the cheek. Then his mother turned to him.

"Is that her? My granddaughter?" His mother's eyes filled with tears.

"Indeed." Emile turned the car seat carrier around so his mother could see the tiny little girl with chubby cheeks and dark hair sleeping soundly. "She apparently likes car rides. She slept so soundly the moment we left Montreal."

His mother leaned over, tears in her eyes. "She's beautiful."

"Let's go inside and you can hold her," Emile suggested.

"I still can't believe you only had her two weeks ago," Marguerite gushed.

"It was a fast birth," Chloé admitted. "She came early and furiously. I had just finished an angioplasty and an hour later I was giving birth on the scrub room floor in Iqaluit. The midwife didn't even have time to get there."

Emile beamed down at his wife. He'd been working in the clinic and barely had time to get there and catch his daughter as she was being born.

"What did you call her again? My apologies, it was hard to hear on the phone when you called and I wanted to make sure that I got her name correctly."

Chloé shared a tender look with him. "Immitaq Marguerite."

His mother brushed away a tear. "I am so happy. So very happy. Let's go inside. I need to hold her."

Chloé wrapped her arm around Marguerite and they headed inside. Emile stared down at his little girl. He never thought he would have a family of his own—he'd thought he'd die alone, just like his father.

He had been on that path.

But here he was. A father, a surgeon, a husband.

It was too much happiness. Something he'd never thought he'd have.

Chloé came back outside. "What're you doing?"

"Just taking it all in." He kissed her quickly. "I love you, Chloé."

"I love you, too, but if we don't take Immi inside to meet her grandmother, your mother will march out here and take our daughter from you."

Emile chuckled. "Good point. Lead on, MacDuff."

Chloé giggled and he wrapped his arm around her, keeping her close. His sunshine, his joy and his love.

* * * * *

If you enjoyed this story, check out these other great reads from Amy Ruttan:

Snowbound with the Single Mom
Their Accidental Vegas Vows
Rebel Doctor's Boston Reunion
Tempted by the Single Dad Next Door

All available now!